THE FORGOTTEN WIDOW'S CHRISTMAS

Victorian Romance

FAYE GODWIN

Tica House
Publishing

Sweet Romance that Delights and Enchants!

PERSONAL WORD FROM THE AUTHOR

DEAREST READERS,

I'm so delighted that you have chosen one of my books to read. I am proud to be a part of the team of writers at Tica House Publishing. Our goal is to inspire, entertain, and give you many hours of reading pleasure. Your kind words and loving readership are deeply appreciated.

I would like to personally invite you to sign up for updates and to become part of our **Exclusive Reader Club**—it's completely Free to Join! I'd love to welcome you!

Much love,

Faye Godwin

**CLICK HERE to Join our Reader's Club and to
Receive Tica House Updates!**

https://victorian.subscribemenow.com/

CONTENTS

PART I

CHAPTER 1

Tilly was breathless with laughter, bent double as she chased after her toddler. Lissa's chubby legs were pumping, her brown curls streaming over her shoulders as she ran, squealing with delight. Her little knitted hat had blown off somewhere in their mad game of tag, but despite the snow crunching under Tilly's feet, she felt a flush of warmth on her cheeks.

"I'm going to get you," she sang out, stretching out her arms toward Lissa.

"No, no," Lissa giggled, dodging left and right. "I'll escape."

"Oh, Lissa, you're so fast." Tilly laughed, carefully measuring her steps to stay a few feet behind the little girl. "I'll never catch you."

Lissa glanced over her shoulder, her cheeks very pink, her eyes as blue as the wintry sky above their heads. They danced with excitement, but glancing back was her mistake. Her tiny shoe caught on a tree root, and she fell headlong and face-first into the snow.

Tilly skidded to a halt, quick to prevent the howling tantrum that might ensue. "Oh, Lissa, look at you," she giggled. "You're playing tag, not making snow angels, you silly girl."

Her light tone worked. Unhurt, Lissa rolled onto her back, snowflakes like stars in her dark hair, eyes shining. "Snow angels," she chuckled, and started waving her arms and legs vigorously in the soft, white powder.

"Snow angels," Tilly announced dramatically, falling onto her back beside Lissa and getting started on one of her own.

"I'm going to make the biggest one," roared four-year-old Robby, throwing himself down beside his mother and waving his limbs madly.

"You're all so silly." Janie, the eldest at six, stomped over to them with her little hands on her hips and a look of great disdain on her long, solemn face. "You can't just change the game right in the middle of playing it."

"Yes, I can," said Lissa, sitting up abruptly. She seized a fistful of snow and flung it at Janie. "Snowball fight!"

The snow hit Janie squarely in the face, and she gasped at the cold. Annoyance flashed over her small features for a second, melting away when she saw Lissa's happy face. "Oh, you're going to be sorry you started it." She giggled, grabbing a handful of snow, and moulding it quickly into a ball.

Utter chaos ensued. Snowballs were flying everywhere; Lissa was running for cover behind the oak tree, Tilly was dithering and wondering which side to join, and Robby was joyously continuing with his snow angel, oblivious to the madness around him. It was several minutes before the children calmed down and they all fell on a heap on the wooden bench under the old oak tree whose great, gnarled limbs stretched over the postage stamp of garden behind their tiny cottage.

Tilly wrapped her arms around the children, hugging them all close. She wondered how long it would be before they were too big to all fit into her arms at once. Although she knew she should be excited for that day – the day when they could start to earn their own keep – her heart longed for days like these to last forever. What could be more perfect than playing with her children on a winter's day like this? And it was a perfect winter's day, with the balmy sunshine making all the snow sparkle, and the cold breeze keeping it all frozen in picturesque, glimmering white.

Lissa, as usual, was the first to wriggle free from Tilly's embrace. "More tag," she demanded, with three-year-old stubbornness.

"Tomorrow, Lissa," said Tilly, smiling. "It'll be cold soon. I think it's time we all went inside and practiced your letters."

"Nooooo," moaned Robby. "I don't want to do letters."

"Well, then you won't be able to write your name on any Christmas cards," said Janie.

Lissa's eyes lit up at once. "Christmas," she cried. "Almost Christmas."

"It's still a few weeks away, my pet." Tilly laughed. "But yes, it's almost Christmas."

Janie took Tilly's hand as they headed for the back door of the cottage. "Will Papa be home for Christmas?" she asked softly.

Tilly looked down at Janie's serious eyes, as dark and shrewd as her father's. "Of course, he will, dear," she said. "Why, he'll be back any minute now." *He had better be*, Tilly thought, a twist of anxiety growing in her stomach.

"What's for supper?" asked Robby.

"Soup," said Tilly.

"Chicken soup?"

"No, my dear. Vegetable soup for tonight."

Robby pouted. "But it's been ages since we had chicken."

Tilly's hand tightened on Janie's. Ray was due back tomorrow, and she had been keeping this a secret from the children; sometimes there were delays, and she didn't want them to be disappointed. But the truth was that the money Ray earned during his voyages was always just enough to tide them through until he returned. If he wasn't home in the next few days, they were going to run out of food.

"We'll have chicken soon," Tilly promised. "And maybe even a roast goose for Christmas – now wouldn't that be nice?"

"Christmas." Lissa giggled, skipping into the tiny kitchen. "I can't wait for Christmas."

TILLY COULD HEAR the children chattering excitedly about the upcoming holiday as she sliced the vegetables for tonight's soup. The little kitchen was scarcely big enough to accommodate her small coal stove, a few cabinets, and the table; but she loved it, for everything was always close at hand.

Except when Ray wanted to talk to her when she was in the kitchen. Then it suddenly felt far too small. He was such a big man, with broad shoulders and bumbling feet, and he was always in the way when she was cooking.

Out of habit, Tilly braced herself for the pang of longing she knew must be coming, that was befitting for a woman whose husband had been at sea for six months. But it didn't come. A dull exhaustion swamped her instead, and an aching emptiness that gnawed at her bones. She was growing more and more acquainted with the dreadful truth that she didn't miss Ray. How could she? They'd been married seven years, and he had never been home for more than two months at a time. He was always out at sea. It felt as though she barely knew him well enough to long for him.

She shook off the disquieting thought and focusing on chopping the turnips nice and fine, to make it look as though there were more of them. Everything would be all right once Ray was home, she told herself. They would soon be having a happy Christmas together, and Tilly would realize she really was still in love with him, wouldn't she?

Things would be clearer then, and she'd be able to buy all the food her children needed and send Janie to school, too. The thought made her smile. She listened to their laughter in the living room, and her heart swelled with love. She told herself again that as long as she had the children, she had everything that she needed.

Tilly was tipping the chopped vegetables into the boiling water when the sound of knocking echoed through the little cottage. Surprised, Tilly wiped her hands on a dishcloth as she moved through the cottage to the front door. Her only visitor was normally her ancient neighbour, who brought biscuits for the children sometimes. But old Polly had already paid her a visit today.

She opened the door and knew instantly something was wrong. The man standing on the doorstep was vaguely familiar: burly, with thickset shoulders and a short neck like a bull's, his black hair streaked with grey and neatly trimmed, his eyes the palest grey, as of the ocean on a misty morning.

"Mr. Carter?" said Tilly hesitantly.

Gold flashed in Bert Carter's smile; it flashed on his lapel too, and at the pocket of his waistcoat, which was beautifully cut from the finest cloth. Bert had been wealthy even before the fleet had started making money hand over fist trading with America.

The smile was brief, though. A mere flickering that never touched his eyes as they traveled slowly across Tilly's body, resting for a moment too long on her chest before they rose to meet her eyes. When they did so, he took off his top hat and pressed it to his chest.

"I beg your pardon for the intrusion, ma'am," he said. "Yes, I am Bert Carter – I own a fleet of ships, as you likely know. Your husband is Raymond Barton, am I correct?"

Tilly's heart hitched in her chest. She glanced past Bert, but there was no sign of Ray.

"Yes," she breathed.

Bert paused. "Ma'am, I'm very sorry," he said, "but I have bad news."

The world seemed to slow down the moment Tilly heard those words. She had always known they were a possibility; had even lived in utter fear and dread of them for the first few years of their marriage. But Ray had come home, over and over again, and Tilly had grown used to the idea that he always would. She had thought this conversation could only happen to other people. Her ears were ringing so loudly she did not hear the words, but she saw the shape of the words leaving Bert's mouth, the way he shook his head, and she knew.

She knew Ray was never coming home.

Somehow, she managed to bid Bert a civil goodbye and to close the door and to walk calmly all the way to her bedroom, to *their* bedroom, and to sit down on the bed and stare at the wall and wait for the floods of tears. Just as the sound of Bert's voice had not been able to penetrate the ringing in her ears, it felt as though the reality could not penetrate her heart.

Raymond's ship was wrecked off the coast of Greenland. There were no survivors.

Ray was gone. Ray was gone. *Ray was gone.* The words beat a steady tattoo on Tilly's heart, but they couldn't get through somehow. It felt like it was happening to someone else.

Then she realized she would have to tell the children.

And that was when she collapsed onto her bed and began to cry.

CHAPTER 2

TILLY WRAPPED her hands around the mug of tea on the kitchen table in front of her. She was shivering, even though old Polly had stoked the fire until it roared in the grate. Polly had brought some wood. Tilly knew how little her elderly, widowed neighbour had to give, but she was glad of the fire now, and wondered how many more days of warmth they had left before their fuel ran out.

Polly was sitting across from her now, her grey head to one side, compassion shining through her milky blue eyes even though the white film over them revealed the fact that she was almost completely blind. She reached over the table, fumbling for a moment before she found Tilly's hand and squeezed it.

"How did the little ones take it?" she asked softly.

Tilly blinked and stared down into her coffee. She hadn't realized she'd been crying until a tear dripped from her cheek and splattered on the wood.

"I don't think they really understand," she said. "Especially not Lissa and Robby. Janie keeps them busy. I... I don't know how much she understands. It's so hard to tell."

"They'll be all right, love," said Polly. "Children are strong little creatures. They'll grow through it. And so will you."

Tilly wasn't so sure. It wasn't the grief that was crushing her, although that was bad enough. It was the regret: all the things she'd never said to Ray, the time she'd never spent with him, the love she'd never had the chance to lavish on him. Having a husband she barely knew had been hard. Losing him was harder. She didn't know how to grieve him, because she was so used to the fact that he was never here; yet somehow the loss of him still ached, still left her feeling off balance each time she thought of the things they would do when Ray got home.

But Ray wasn't coming home. And to Tilly, that meant a far greater weight than just her grief and regret.

"I don't see how we can grow through this, Polly," she said, her voice hitching. "I don't even see how we can survive this."

Polly immediately understood. She squeezed her hands tightly. "I'll help you in any way that I can, deary. I... I wish I had more to give you."

"You've already been an angel to me," Tilly sobbed, the tears overwhelming her. "I know you can hardly eat yourself, but you've been giving us bits of food... and... and that's the only way the children and I have survived the past week, and with holding Ray's funeral... with nothing of him to bury... oh... Polly."

Tilly began to sob, and Polly leaned over the table and hugged her awkwardly, allowing Tilly to weep on her shoulder. It felt as though the very earth had been yanked out from under Tilly's feet. She didn't know what to do, where to turn, how to feed her children tomorrow.

"Now, now, my love," said Polly, gently but firmly. "You're going to be all right, but you have to sit up now and dry your eyes and face what you have to do."

Polly's compassionate firmness helped Tilly to do as she said. She wiped at her eyes, looking desperately at the old woman.

"What can I do?" she whispered. "I... I need to find work. But where do I begin? I have no references, no experience." She had been only seventeen when she'd married Ray.

"You have plenty of experience," said Polly. "You've raised three children, my lamb. But let's set that aside for now. You may not need it right away." She spread her hands. "Ray must still be due some money for the journey he made – perhaps more because he died in it. You'd have to find out from his employer."

"From Bert Carter?" said Tilly.

"That's right. You need to go to him, Tilly, and ask for Ray's payment. That would be enough to tide you over for a while at least, until you can find your feet. Maybe longer – depending on his arrangement with Mr. Carter."

Tilly hadn't known anything about Ray's work, let alone the details of what would happen if he was lost at sea. She'd never thought it would happen to them. The thought that there might be some money for them after all hadn't occurred to her, and she was grateful Polly had brought it up.

"Maybe things are going to be a little easier than I thought," she said.

"Maybe, my darling." Polly squeezed her hands. "Keep your chin up now, pet. You'll find a strength you never knew you had, for your children's sake."

Tilly would later realize that Polly was absolutely right.

I⊤ WAS an hour's walk through the snowy streets from Tilly's cottage to the offices of Carter Fleet, and Tilly was tired and breathless by the time she walked up to the large, imposing building by the docks. It was all glass doorways with bronze lettering on the doors and rich, expensive carpeting inside, and Tilly's heart was pounding when she walked up to the glass. There were no women inside, she saw, only what seemed like hundreds of men sitting at desks, talking with one another, and scribbling in books. They were all wearing suits. None of them looked like sailors. Tilly wondered if a woman had ever stepped inside this building.

Part of her expected she would be thrown out the moment she stepped through the doors. Indeed, an appalled hush did fall on the room, and suddenly all the men were staring at her. Some were watching her with gaping jaws, their expensive pipes hanging loosely over their lips.

"Um, excuse me," Tilly said, her voice very small and pathetic in the huge room. "I'm here to see Mr. Carter."

A smarmy young secretary leaped up from his desk near the door and hastened to her side. "Mr. Carter is only available by appointment, ma'am," he said, putting a gentle but irresistible hand on her arm. "We kindly request for you to leave. Perhaps your husband can send Mr. Carter a wire requesting a meeting with him."

Tilly wanted nothing more than to flee this room, but she thought of her children with panic and dug in her heels. "No, no, you don't understand." she said. "I don't have a husband. He..."

"Please, ma'am, I must insist," said the secretary. "You need to leave."

"But I have to talk to Mr. Carter," cried Tilly. "My husband was lost at sea, and..."

"Bogsworth." called a sharp voice from the far side of the room. "Is that any way to treat a lovely young widow?"

The secretary immediately let go of Tilly, as though her skin had suddenly turned to acid. She turned to see Bert Carter standing in a doorway at the back of the room. His eyes flashed over her, and his features relaxed into a sympathetic smile.

"What are you all staring at?" he demanded of the men who were still gaping at her.

"Sir, she has made no appointment," protested Bogsworth.

"She has just lost her husband on one of our ships, young man," said Bert very firmly. "She needs no appointment. Dear Mrs. Barton, please step into my office. I believe we have much to discuss."

A surge of inexpressible relief rushed through Tilly, and she scampered across the floor and into Bert's office with a sigh. The office was huge, with thick carpeting and a huge fire crackling in the hearth; a string of mistletoe hung on the mantelpiece, and there was a wreath on the door. Bert had wasted no time in getting started on his Christmas decorations. It was deliciously warm and cosy after the freezing wind on the street.

"Please, take a seat," said Bert, opening a drinks cabinet behind his desk.

Tilly sank gratefully into a deep leather chair on the other side of Bert's desk. He produced a crystal decanter and two glasses, sloshing a generous amount of some amber-colored liquid into them. "Here," he said. "It'll warm you up."

Tilly had never drunk alcohol before, but she didn't want to be rude to the man who could be her children's salvation. She took a polite sip and pressed her lips together to keep from spluttering as the liquid burned all the way into her stomach.

"I've come to see you about my husband, sir," she said.

"As I'm sure you have," said Bert warmly. He sat down and took a generous gulp from his own glass, despite the fact that it was three o' clock on a Wednesday afternoon. "Raymond was an excellent sailor, Mrs. Barton. You can be very proud of him."

A twinge of pride, indeed, touched Tilly's heart, but it was filled with sorrow. She hadn't known that his colleagues held him in such high esteem. In fact, she had barely known anything about the husband she'd just lost.

"Thank you, sir," she said, forcing herself to stay focused. "He was a good husband, too, and father."

"Oh, you have children?" said Bert.

"Yes, three." Tilly's voice cracked a little. "Janie is six, Robert is four, and Lissa is three."

"How lovely." Bert had a warm, welcoming smile. "They must bring you great joy." Wistfulness came into his eyes, and Tilly noticed that there was a small, framed photograph on his desk of a smiling girl.

"Do you have children, sir?" she asked, grasping at any straw she could find to win even more of the big man's sympathy.

"A little girl. Darcy," said Bert. "The light of my life."

"Then you understand how it is to be a parent." Tilly leaned forward, allowing her desperation to leak into her voice. "Sir, I'm a widow now, and with three little mouths to feed at home. I've never worked before. I have an education, but no references, and nowhere to start looking for a job. We were counting on Ray's payment to come in over the next week or so." Tears filled her eyes. "But now we have nothing. I can't even buy my children food or a little candle to light the window for Christmas. Oh, please, sir, tell me that there was some arrangement for us to get a little money if Ray died at sea. Please, tell me there's a pension or an allowance or – or just the payment from his last voyage." She covered her face with her hands and began to cry hopelessly.

"Now, now, Mrs. Barton – may I call you Matilda?" said Bert.

"Tilly, please," she choked out.

"Now then, Tilly, it's going to be all right." Bert produced a perfectly folded, monogrammed handkerchief from his pocket and gave it to her with a little flourish. She took it and dabbed at her eyes, her free hand lying on the desk. To her surprise, Bert reached over and placed his big hand over hers. It was surprisingly cold for the warmth of the room.

"You must think me such a fool," Tilly sobbed.

"Not at all. You've been through something awful, you poor thing," said Bert. "And I do want to help you in any way that I can, Tilly... *if* I can."

The inflection in those last three words stopped her in her tracks. She was just beginning to think Bert was going to help them after all, and now she wasn't sure. She raised her face, swallowing her tears.

"Wh-what do you mean?" she stammered.

Bert held up one hand in a helpless gesture, keeping the other resting on hers. "Well, you must understand that I've had a terrible financial blow myself," he said. "The ship was lost with all of her cargo, and of course, the only way I can pay the crew is to deliver the cargo." He shrugged. "With the cargo lost, not to mention the devastating loss of the ship, well, there's just no payment for Raymond this time."

His words struck a terrible chill to the pit of Tilly's stomach. "And – and was there no – no allowance for... us?" she stammered out, the sobs threatening to overwhelm her once more.

"None, I'm afraid. Raymond must have lacked the foresight to put money aside for his family." Bert cocked his head, giving her a sympathetic little smile. "I'm sorry, Tilly, but there may be nothing I can do for you."

"May be?" Tilly breathed, her hammering heart clutching at the faint possibility in those words.

"Well... I wouldn't say this to just any widow, you know," said Bert. His grip on her hand changed, tightened, and Tilly wasn't sure she liked it. When he leaned over the desk, she saw there were tiny beads of sweat at his hairline. "But perhaps you and I could come to an... arrangement."

His meaning was unmistakable even before he raised his free hand and caressed her cheek with the back of his index finger. The touch grated across her, like nails down a blackboard, and Tilly whipped her hand and face out of his reach before she could think.

"Sir," she cried.

"Now, now, don't be skittish, Tilly," said Bert smoothly, easily recapturing her hand in both of his own. "You're a beautiful woman. I certainly would love to help you, if you could give me a few... little favours in exchange."

His eyes glided over her chest as he spoke, and Tilly knew exactly what he meant. Suddenly his hands were very clammy over hers. She pulled it away, leaping out of her chair.

"Sir, I..."

"Don't be a fool, Tilly." Bert's voice was still calm, but there was a hint of steel in it now. "You know the position you're in. You need my money." He shrugged, his eyes wandering again. "And I need something from you, too."

The blood was rushing in Tilly's ears. Had he locked the door behind her? Suddenly the warmth and cosiness of the office had become suffocating. If she screamed, would any of those men outside, men whose pockets were lined with Bert's money, come running to help her?

She inched toward the door. Bert got up from his desk, his eyes watching her levelly.

"Stop and think," he said again. "Isn't this the easy way out?"

Tilly couldn't fathom doing what he wanted. He was married. He had a daughter. How could he even dream of asking this from her? She had just lost her own husband, and now he wanted to force himself upon her?

"Tilly," said Bert, "don't – "

Tilly wheeled around and bolted, yanking at the door. For a horrible instant, she thought he was right behind her, ready to grab her. But nothing seized her, the door swung open, and then she was running, right across the entrance room, hearing shouts and surprised oaths from the men, caring for nothing except the glass door at the far end. It swung open when she slammed into it and then she was breathing the blessedly cold air of the street and running down the pavement as fast as her legs could carry her.

Bert did not pursue her. But she still ran another three blocks, just to be sure.

CHAPTER 3

TILLY'S FEET crunched in the snow with each step, the cold sapping her strength. She had always loved days like this one, with the sky a soft grey, the clouds feeling so close she could reach up and touch their fluffiness, and beautiful snowflakes tumbling slowly down in profusion. It was inexpressibly beautiful, especially this close to Christmas. Every house Tilly passed was decorated more extravagantly than the one before: there were strings of bunting hanging from window to window, great, colourful wreaths on every door, blazing golden candlelight in every window. They all had Christmas trees out on the front lawn; some had more than one, decked out with candles and ribbons and bright sprigs of holly.

Today, the beauty seemed somehow cruel to Tilly. She was wearing her best coat, but the bitter cold still penetrated through it as the afternoon faded toward evening. The snow made it harder to walk, and her aching limbs had traversed many a bitter mile today already.

Ray was usually home for Christmas, if only for a few weeks. He would always take the children off to the woods and cut down a little tree to carry home, which they would set up in their tiny kitchen and drape with paper chains and ginger-bread figures that Tilly would bake and ice with the help of the two girls. Last year, Lissa had put her thumb clumsily into the middle of Janie's meticulously iced gingerbread camel. Tilly had expected a meltdown, but instead Janie had calmly told her little sister that the camel was now just perfect. Ray had been so proud of her, so surprised at how quickly his little girl was growing up.

Now he would never see her become the young woman Tilly saw in her. She swallowed hard, not wanting to cry. The tears would only chill her cheeks all the more.

Turning off the pavement, Tilly trudged through the knee-deep snow accumulating on a narrow path up to the servants' entrance of one of the manor houses. She passed under the shadow of an extravagant Christmas tree, trying to draw hope from its splendour as she reached the back door and peered through the kitchen window. Even here, there were Christmas decorations among the utilitarian simplicity of the kitchen: a candle here, a Christmas card on a mantelpiece there, a wreath on the back door, dusted with picturesque snow.

She knocked, making some of the snowflake down from the wreath. It was a few minutes before the door swung open, and a harassed, red-faced woman glared down at her. Her eyes glanced over Tilly's clothing, which was still quite neat – a fact which Tilly knew was the only thing stopping this house-keeper from chasing her right off the grounds immediately.

"Yes?" she said sharply.

"Good afternoon, ma'am," said Tilly, trying desperately to sound as educated as she could. "I'm looking for work – I've been a housewife for years, and I know cooking, cleaning, laundry, caring for children..."

"We have no posts available," said the woman icily. "Good day."

She slammed the door, leaving Tilly staring at the wreath, which swung and bumped with the force of it. Tilly blinked, feeling as though she'd just been slapped. The housekeeper hadn't even given her a chance to finish talking. It was hard not to let her sorrow turn to bitterness in her chest.

She turned away and stared into the cold, grey day. Polly had been talking to everyone she knew, but the little old blind lady hardly left her cottage anymore; Tilly even did her shop-ping for her. She hardly knew anyone. None of Tilly's contacts had been helpful, either. She had been trudging door to door for weeks now, and the bit of money she had left was rapidly running out.

She didn't know what she'd give the children for breakfast tomorrow morning. An icy fear clutched at her, as though the frost itself had grown fingers and dug them into her heart.

She took a long, shaky breath. There was no time for fear. She had to press on.

For the children.

❦

TILLY'S HEAD had been aching even before Lissa had started crying, and that was two hours ago. Now, it was pounding, as though someone was inside her skull searing the back of her eyes with a hot poker. She squinted in the candlelight, trying to focus on the shirt that lay across her lap. It was an insufficient, flickering light, but it had been weeks since Tilly had been able to afford gas.

She threaded a needle, squinting down at the shirt. She had just cut a new patch for it, and she promised herself that if she could just finish this shirt, she would put the children to bed.

There was a thunder of footsteps coming down the short hallway, and Janie burst into the kitchen where Tilly was sitting. The little girl's face was pale in the semi-darkness.

"I can't get her to stop, Mama," she cried. "She just won't stop."

Tilly sighed, starting the first stitch. "I'll be there in a minute, Janie."

"She won't stop," Janie whimpered, a few tears sliding down her cheeks. "She's hungry. We're all hungry."

Janie's piping little voice broke on the last syllable, and Tilly closed her eyes, forcing herself not to cry. How could she leave her six-year-old alone with a screaming three-year-old? The church bell struck ten o' clock; Tilly knew the children should have been asleep long ago, but she had gotten a whole basket of mending from their wealthier neighbour down the street, and she knew that if she didn't finish it all by early tomorrow morning then there wouldn't be any money for lunchtime. There was already nothing for breakfast, and she'd given each child only one slice of bread tonight.

She focused on thinking about food and coal and candles. She couldn't let herself think about the looming spectre of rent that towered over them all like a deadly shadow.

"I'm coming, Janie," she said softly, laying down the shirt. "Go and wash your face, and I'll put you to bed."

Janie's tense little shoulders relaxed a little, and she headed obediently for the little washroom. Tilly followed Lissa's howls to the room the children shared. It was still bright and freshly painted from the last time Ray had come back from a voyage, but it looked dingy now in the fading light of a single candle stub.

"Mama." shrieked Lissa, who was in the midst of a full-blown tantrum on the bedroom floor. "I'm HUNGRY."

Her cry reached an ear-splitting pitch, and Tilly gritted her teeth over the wave of helpless, exhausted rage that washed through her. She knelt next to the little girl, fighting back her tears of guilt and tiredness.

"Lissy, my sweetheart," she murmured, scooping her toddler into her arms. "Hush now. Hush."

"Hungry," Lissa moaned, but her little body was trembling with exhaustion. She had just about cried herself out.

"Sleep now, baby," Tilly whispered. She straightened, carrying Lissa to the double bed that the children shared. "Just sleep now, and we'll have plenty to eat in the morning."

She knew that this would only be true if she could work through the night, but if she could bring a smile to this little girl's face, it would be worth it. She hated the boniness she felt as she held her once-chubby toddler, hated the way Lissa's shoulders shuddered with exhausted sobs. Curling up on the bed − Robby was a sleeping heap at one end, somehow sleeping through his sister's screams − she wrapped herself around Lissa and held her, stroking her dirty hair. There had been no money for soap for a few days now.

"Hush," she soothed. "Hush, my little one."

Tears trickled down Tilly's cheeks as she cradled her child, at the same time desperate not to rise from this bed and not to let her go, but just as desperate for Lissa to fall asleep so that she could go back to work. She squeezed her eyes shut for a moment, kissing Lissa on the forehead.

She had never felt so alone in her life.

TILLY DIDN'T KNOW what she would do without Polly this Christmas. The old lady always went off to visit her sister in the country at Christmastime, and even though Polly had offered to stay home and help Tilly with the children this year, Tilly hadn't been able to accept that sweet offer. She knew Polly lived for her visits with her sister – and that she didn't have many years left in which to enjoy them.

At least Polly was watching the children for one more day today before leaving for the country, and Tilly was hastening through the streets back toward the cottage, her arms bless-edly full of brown paper bags containing yesterday's bread, slightly wrinkled vegetables, and a somewhat questionable string of sausages. Her children could eat a hot meal tonight and maybe tomorrow, too, and for now that was all Tilly wanted.

She was just starting to relax slightly as she turned into her street when she spotted him: a portly, pleasant figure that she would normally be glad to see, but that struck shock and fear into her heart right now. It was Mr. Jones, her landlord. He was a agreeable fellow, but Tilly had been avoiding him for three weeks now. She just didn't have the money for rent.

Tilly stopped in her tracks, glancing around madly from one holly-strewn doorway to the next. She had just decided to dive down an alley between two houses when she heard Mr. Jones' cheerful voice.

"Hello, Mrs. Barton," he cried. "Merry Christmas."

She couldn't avoid him now. He sounded friendly enough, so perhaps she could somehow convince him to give her one more week, even though she knew from other neighbors that Mr. Jones' friendliness quickly ran out when it came to non-payment. Gritting her teeth, she turned to face the short man who was hastening up the street toward her.

"Mr. Jones," she said, painfully feigning surprise. "How nice it is to see you." Inside, she was dying.

Mr. Jones was slightly breathless when he caught up with her. "It seems like we're going to have a cold Christmas," he said conversationally.

Tilly searched his eyes. Was he building up to telling her that they were evicted? She thought of her children out on the streets, and her heart was suddenly beating in all the wrong places.

"It does seem that way, sir," she quavered.

"I would wish you a merry Christmas, but I fear my words would be greatly misplaced, Mrs. Barton." Mr. Jones laid a hand on her arm. After Bert's unwelcome touch, it was all Tilly could do not to flinch, but there was only genuine friendliness in Mr. Jones' eyes. "I was so very sorry to hear about Mr. Barton being lost at sea. What a terrible fate for a young woman and three little ones to lose the man of the house in that way."

Tilly fought to hold back her tears. He seemed so kind, but any minute now, he would bring up the subject of the rent. "Thank you, sir."

"I'm pleased that the fleet has been taking care of you, though." Mr. Jones let his hand fall to his side. "Sometimes these companies don't care at all about the poor men who are lost with their ships."

Tilly blinked at him. "Sir?"

"I just think it's a good thing they're paying your expenses, that's all." Mr. Jones paused. "It was the Carter fleet that Mr. Barton worked for, wasn't it?"

"That's right," said Tilly, "but I... I'm afraid I don't quite understand what you mean."

"Why, Tilly, they've been paying your rent for two weeks now," said Mr. Jones. "And caught you up on all of your outstanding payments, too. Such a pleasant chap it was that came to see me at my office, too. Bert, I think it was – Bert

Carter, the owner himself. How kind of him to concern himself with you, when he has so many other things to worry about."

Tilly dearly wanted to be relieved at Mr. Jones' words, but she was far from it. She was terrified, her bones turning to ice where she stood. Why was Bert paying her rent? She'd refused his advances and expected never to hear from him again. Her heart was pounding, and she tried to talk herself into believing that he'd had a change of heart, that he was willing to help her now even though she had rejected him.

"Mrs. Barton, are you quite all right?" said Mr. Jones worriedly.

"I... I must be on my way," Tilly stammered. "E-excuse me."

Clutching her paper bags tightly to her chest, Tilly stumbled off toward home, her heart thundering in her ears. She wished she could believe Bert was doing this out of the kindness of his heart.

But she wasn't sure Bert Carter had a heart to begin with.

CHAPTER 4

TILLY KNEW that finding work this close to Christmas would be practically impossible. Even the mending had started to dry up now; her client down the street had gone off to Lancaster to visit her family, and Polly had gone to her sister's, and now there was no one in London who cared about them at all. No one but Bert Carter, who had been paying the rent all along, and Tilly wasn't sure that 'caring' was a word she would have used to describe him.

She tried not to think about him. She had other things to think about, even though he had been haunting her every thought. Most pressing of all was the fact that she had a sixpence in her pocket, and that was all. It would buy them enough bread to survive for today, but what of tomorrow? A week before Christmas, and Tilly had nothing.

"You have to be good now, children," she said, trying to keep her hands from shaking as she buttoned Lissa's coat. "Don't go outside, and don't open the door to anyone you don't know. Do you understand, Janie?"

Janie was watching her with sad, solemn eyes. She didn't look six years old anymore, Tilly thought. She looked like an old, old woman. "Mama, why do you have to go?" she whispered, her eyes pleading.

"Honey, you know why," sighed Tilly. "I have to find work."

"But why? You never worked before," Robby chipped in.

"Mama has to find work so that we can have money for food and such things," said Tilly, fighting her tears.

Robby dropped his eyes. There were dark circles under them; she wondered when last her little son had gone to sleep on a full stomach and slept knowing there would be enough to eat tomorrow.

"I don't want you to go," he mumbled.

"Me neither." Janie snatched at Tilly's skirt. "Please, Mama, please, don't go. We want you here with us." Her eyes filled with tears. "You never play with us anymore."

"Mama has to go." Tilly blinked back her tears, disentangling Janie's hands from her skirt. "I'll bring food tonight, I promise. Please, just stay in the house and wait for me to get back."

"I want Polly," moaned Lissa.

Tilly wanted Polly, too, but wanting was no good.

"I'm hungry," wailed Janie.

"Drink some water," said Tilly desperately. "It'll fill your bellies." It was a lie, of course. She had tried it herself several times when there had been enough food for the children, but not for her. All the water did was made her feel sick.

She somehow managed to pry herself away from Janie and shut the door in her children's faces. She could hear them crying as she turned and trudged up the street, their wails pursuing her with every step she took. Bitter tears coursed down her cheeks. Tilly made no attempt to stop them. She knew she had already failed her children, but somehow, she had to make it right.

The only way she could think to do that was to find work. Gritting her teeth, she set off into the wind, which hurled fistfuls of snowflakes that sliced through her clothing like so many tiny knives. She'd sold all her good coats for food, and now she struggled to draw her tattered shawl around her, shivering in the teeth of the wind.

By the time she neared the end of the street, she could still hear Lissa's shrieking. She hesitated then, wanting with all of her heart to go back, to cradle her child in her arms, to cuddle with them in the comparative warmth of their dark little cottage. It would be so appealing to give up. So appealing to wrap them all in her arms, and curl up in bed, and just let fate do with them what it would.

Tilly squared her shoulders, though it seemed to take the last ounces of her strength. She couldn't do that. She had to feed her children. She set off again, the wind blasting in her face, whipping her tears away into the frigid morning.

IT TOOK ALL of Tilly's strength not to reach into the paper bag she was carrying in her arms. The bread inside was stale, but its scent still wafted up to meet her. The wild morning had turned into a quiet, dark evening. The cold, slow and insidious, was biting into Tilly's bones despite her attempts to walk briskly. Her breath curled around her face as steam, and with each breath, she could smell that bread.

When had she last eaten? Yesterday, maybe? Tilly couldn't remember. All she knew was that she was fighting to keep her hands from slipping inside, tearing off just a tiny bit of the bread, and wolfing it down. She knew that if she gave in, she would collapse here and finish it all, and there would be nothing left for the children.

Taking deep breaths, Tilly paused on the turn to her cottage, taking the time to rally all of her willpower. She knew what scene would meet her once she reached the cottage. Lissa would probably still be in a screaming tantrum; Robby withdrawn in some corner; Janie tearful and desperate. They would tear the bread apart in moments, their manners forgotten in the face of starvation. Then Lissa would scream for more, and they'd all go to bed still hungry.

But she had to face it, she had to get through this evening, and the next, and the next. So she steeled herself and walked down the street.

There were no screams or cries coming from her cottage. Tilly felt relief for a moment, then a bolt of terror shot through her. Were the children still home? Had they gone out, as she'd forbidden them to do? Her limbs found strength in fear, and she broke into a jog.

Tilly was halfway down the street when she heard it. Robby's voice. Sobbing – or was it sobbing? Her stride faltered, and she slowed to a walk, listening incredulously.

Robby wasn't sobbing: he was laughing, laughing in a way she hadn't heard him laugh since that last happy day when they'd made snow angels under the tree in the garden.

Tilly couldn't fathom what reason her little boy had found to laugh like this, but she savoured it, slowing down to a walk, closing her eyes and listening to that glorious, musical sound. He'd had an adorable laugh since he was a baby, and it was one of the loveliest things Tilly had ever heard, rippling and dancing through the air. Somehow all the candles in the windows shone brighter, the holly berries were redder, the very air seemed warmer and more filled with the promise of Christmas.

Tilly was almost smiling by the time she reached the front door. She heard happy voices inside now, Janie giggling, Lissa talking, Robby interjecting from time to time. Pushing the door open, she found it in her to raise her voice in a happy tone, too.

"Children," she called. "I'm home, my darlings."

She stepped into the kitchen, and her happy heart froze instantly in her chest, as though a frigid blast from the north had turned it to ice. Bert Carter was standing in the kitchen.

For a long, slow moment, Tilly couldn't move or breathe. He was right there in his top hat and tailcoat, his fine hair shining under the light of a gas lamp – and when last had they been able to afford gas for the lights? A laugh had transfigured his face, and he was holding a bright silver pound in his hand. It was more money than Tilly had held in a long time.

"Oh. And it's gone again," Bert said, breaking eye contact and making the coin disappear with a flick of his wrist. "But what's this? Why, I dare say..." He reached out toward Janie, touching behind her ear, and, with another flick, the coin reappeared in his hand.

The children burst into fits of wondering laughter. Janie grinned up at Bert, her mouth smeared with chocolate. Chocolate? Tilly blinked. The kitchen table was laden with half-eaten food: a plate of sticky buns littered with crumbs, one half of a rabbit pie, orange peels lying everywhere. Each child had a mug of chocolate in front of them.

"Mama," cried Lissa, jumping down from her stool and rushing over to Tilly. She threw her arms around Tilly's leg and looked up at her, giggling, her eyes dancing.

"Hello, sweetheart," Tilly stammered out. Despite her terror, she could feel part of herself melting at the sight of Lissa's smile. When last had she seen her children so happy?

"There's food, Mama." Janie grabbed a sticky bun and held it out to Tilly, her eyes wide. "Eat."

Tilly wanted, more than anything, to snatch that bun from Janie's hand and devour it. But her eyes were dragged back to Bert's, to the smugness in them, and fear chewed at her soul.

"Mr. Carter," she said, ignoring the heart-breaking confusion on Janie's face.

"Mrs. Barton." Bert smiled. "Please, take a seat. Have a slice of pie – and some chocolate."

Tilly's hands were shaking. He was so close to her children. She stumbled into a seat, and he thrust a plate of pie toward her.

"Mr. Carter bought loads of food, Mama," said Robby, his eyes shining.

"Mama, why aren't you eating?" cried Janie.

"Hush," said Tilly. Her voice trembled.

"Janie, Robby, Lissa." Bert bent down, hands on his knees, and grinned at the children. "Why don't you run along to the sitting room and finish drinking your chocolate there? Then your mama and I can have a little... talk." The inflection of his words sent a terrible chill all the way down Tilly's spine.

"All right," said Janie meekly. She picked up her and Lissa's mugs. "Come on. Let's go."

The children trooped out, and Tilly wasn't sure whether to feel relieved or even more frightened. She turned her eyes to Bert, who took a seat at the table as though he'd been welcomed there. He took Ray's seat. Tilly hated him for it.

"Your children are simply delightful, Tilly," he said. "I do love them – especially the little one. She has your eyes." His smile was predatory. Tilly remembered the way his fingertips had brushed Janie's ear, and goosebumps scattered on her body.

"Please," she quavered. "Please, whatever you do, don't harm my children."

"Now why in the world would I want to do that?" Bert shook his head. "You think me a monster, Matilda. Please. Have a bite of that pie."

Tilly didn't want to anger him. She lifted a fork, her hand shaking so that it rattled on the plate, and took a bite of the pie. The flavours were delicious – she couldn't remember when last she'd had real meat like this, flavourful and wholesome – but it turned to cardboard in her mouth, and she gagged it down as Bert smiled at her.

"I'm not here to hurt your children," he said, his voice warm and deep and chilling. "I'm not here to hurt anyone at all. I'm just here to remind you that all of your troubles could effortlessly go away... and you'd hardly have to do a thing."

He leaned over the table and put his hand over hers again. The flinch ran the length of Tilly's body, but she forced herself to stay still. For an instant, with the smell of rabbit pie in her nose and the laughter of her children in her ears, she considered it. She considered giving in. It would be so easy. It could be her secret. But what then? What would she become? A kept woman? What would her children become?

She screwed up her courage and pulled her hand away. "I think you should leave," she quavered.

Bert's eyes flashed, and it was as though a curtain was lifted, as though a mask fell away to give Tilly a chilling glimpse of what lay behind his affable smile.

"Use your head, woman," he growled. "What other choices do you have? You will never find work in this city. You're only a girl. There's just one thing you could do well, and that's all I ask of you."

Tilly had never felt so demeaned, so reduced to nothing but a body, a soulless shell designed only for another's pleasure. It gave her a flash of anger, just enough to get to her feet and step toward the door.

"Please," she said, her voice still trembling. "Just leave."

Bert got to his feet. His fists were clenched on the kitchen table, on *her* kitchen table. "You'll regret this," he snarled, but he began to move toward the door.

He would have to pass right by her to leave. Tilly screwed her eyes shut when he approached. Maybe he would walk past. Maybe the nightmare was over. But instead, Bert paused, so close that she felt his breath, felt the heat radiating from his body mere inches from her own.

"You're an imbecile, woman," he whispered, "but your fire won't stop me. It only makes me long for you even more." He leaned closer, his lips brushing her ear as he spoke, making her shake. "You will give in, sooner or later. For your sake, it had better be sooner, or you will learn a hard lesson about the consequences of refusing me."

Tilly opened her eyes. He was so close, so overwhelmingly near, so hulking, and she was trapped. She blurted out the first thing that came to her mind.

"I'll write to your wife," she spat. "I'll tell her what you're doing."

His eyes were as cold as the night air outside now. He leaned closer, his voice a low growl that chilled her to the bones.

"I wouldn't do that if I were you," he snarled. "I know where you live."

Tilly couldn't hold back a sob of utter fear. Bert leaned closer then, and kissed her resisting lips for a long instant, tasting of booze and sweat and violation. Then he turned and strode away into the night, and Tilly slammed and bolted the door behind him, sliding down to the floor with sobs of helpless terror, her hands cupped over her mouth so that her children would not hear.

CHAPTER 5

TILLY GLANCED OVER HER SHOULDER, first this way, then that way. Twilight was falling swiftly, the street lit up by street lamps and made doubly bright by the Christmas decorations on every door and window, the wreaths and strings of mistletoe hanging from every lamppost. The beauty was lost on Tilly tonight, though. Instead, her eyes sought out the shadows, prying into the depths of each one.

"Mama, can we go home?" Janie asked softly.

Tilly glanced down at the children. Lissa was clinging to her skirt with one hand and sucking her thumb with the other, her eyes vacant. Robby had sat down in a heap on the pavement in the few seconds that Tilly had been standing still. Janie had a bundle of dirty clothes in her arms. Some kind old lady had sent them to Tilly to be washed for a precious few pennies, which was a good thing; the food Bert had brought a few days ago had run out. Tilly hadn't been able to touch any of it herself, but how could she deny her children the opportunity to fill their bellies, even knowing the man that had brought that food was evil to the core?

"In a minute," said Tilly, clutching a basket of clothes for mending a little tighter. She turned and looked back once more, sweeping the street with desperate eyes.

She wasn't sure what she was looking for. Bert himself, perhaps, sheltering in a dark doorway, those eyes of his trained upon her. Maybe one of his men, loitering nonchalantly, watching her every move to tell Bert her routines. She had been trying to break them up, going out early one morning and late the next, popping home at midday only to head out again. But she still had the feeling, every moment, that someone was right behind her.

"Mama," Janie croaked.

Tilly relented. She didn't know how many miles they had walked today, knocking on door after door in search of work, but she knew that her children were utterly exhausted and half-starved to boot. Lissa's nose was very red, her frame shivering in the winter air. Robby seemed past caring. His head was pillowed on his arms where they were crossed over his drawn-up knees.

"Let's go," she said softly. "Come on, Robby."

"Come on." Janie plucked at Robby's sleeve.

The boy somehow got to his feet, and they all staggered down the street to the dark cottage; the gas Bert had paid for had run out, too. Tilly wondered vaguely if he'd paid the rent this week. She wasn't sure what to hope for, and her brain was too occupied with fear to worry about that right now. Unlocking the door, she pushed it open and groped instantly for the candle and tinderbox in the niche by the door. Robby started to push past her into the room, and she jammed a foot across the doorway, stopping him.

"No," she shouted. "Don't push."

Robby looked up at her with round, shocked eyes, and Tilly regretted the tone of her voice but said nothing. Setting down the basket, she lit a candle and held it aloft. The light chased shadows that all seemed to be sneering at her, but the kitchen was empty.

"Stay here," she ordered, setting the candle on the kitchen table and locking the door behind the children.

"Mama, I want to go to bed," whined Lissa.

"I said to stay here," Tilly shouted.

Her voice reverberated around the kitchen, and the children fell utterly silent, watching her with huge eyes as she grabbed another candle from the mantelpiece. This one was little more than a stub, but it provided a faint light. Leaving the children in the small bubble of golden safety cast by the first candle, Tilly moved through the rest of the house, shining the little light in every corner, seeing lurkers in every shadow. She was still shaking when she returned to the kitchen, even though there had been nothing in the house. She did not have the courage to go out into the garden.

"We're hungry, Mama," Janie whimpered as she came into the kitchen.

Tilly wished she hadn't shouted at them, but she didn't have the energy to apologize.

"Let's eat, then," she said.

Janie produced from her pocket a small packet of cold chips. Tilly counted the chips and divided them equally among the children, then took two for herself. They were gone so quickly. There was no firewood left. She put the children to bed in their clothes, bundling all of the blankets they owned around them, and waited for their breathing to grow low and deep.

But Tilly herself did not get into the bed with them. She sat on the foot of the bed, staring out of the bedroom window that looked into the back garden. So many times, she had enjoyed sitting here, watching the birds flitting around the branches of the old tree, enjoying the brightness of the flowers blooming along the wall, listening to the song of rain on the roof. Now, her eyes sought to pierce the thick dark- ness. Was that a figure against the back wall? Was that movement just a branch in the wind, or something far more sinister?

She didn't know. So she watched, and she watched.

SOMEONE WAS AT THE WINDOW.

Tilly jerked awake, utterly certain of it. Her neck and back ached; she had fallen asleep propped against the bedstead. She had no idea how long she had slept, but the house was in utter darkness.

And someone was trying to get in through the window.

She could hear the scratching, the tapping of their fingernails as they looked for the latch, and her heart was hammering in her throat. Slowly, she rose to her feet, groping for the candle that had been on the nightstand. Her fingers found only a pool of molten wax; there was no wick left. The candle was spent. The other candle was still in the kitchen, blown out.

Tilly's heart pounded so hard that she felt it in her wrists, in her feet. The scratching continued, a dull thump as the intruder stumbled around outside. The wind had a desolate edge to it as it howled around the corners of the cottage like a mournful spirit locked out of its grave, seeking, seeking a way in with its cold fingers. The children were sleeping. Were they safe? What could she do? She looked around the dark room for a weapon, even though her eyes could not hope to penetrate the blackness. She seized the empty candlestick from the nightstand. Rising to her feet, Tilly clutched the candlestick in two uncontrollably trembling hands. She would swing it if she had to. If something came through that window.

For an interminable few minutes, Tilly stood trembling by the foot of the bed, ready to do battle for the sake of her children. Anxiety burned in the pit of her stomach, a nausea born of fear clutching at her throat. It was only when a few more minutes had passed, and Tilly's sleep-addled brain began to rationalize what she was seeing, that she realized that nothing had come through the window yet. Surely groping fingers would have found the latch by now?

But she could still hear it, the scratching, the rattling of some-thing at the window. She knew that something was there. Why wasn't it coming in? Was it meant to be a distraction? The thought sent a lance of cold fear up her spine, and she whirled to face the bedroom door, which was open and seemed to yawn into the blackness of the hallway. Rushing to it, Tilly yanked it shut, and the rattling at the window intensi-fied. Something was coming. She whirled around with the candlestick raised over her shoulder, waiting, but nothing came.

Her heart was beating right out of her chest. Shaking, Tilly tiptoed toward the window. Maybe she should yank it open and strike first. She didn't know, but she couldn't stand here and watch for a moment longer. Summoning the last remnants of her courage, Tilly flung the window wide open, the candlestick over her shoulder, ready to strike –

The wind howled, hurling snow against her face with burning cold. Tilly gasped with the cold, blinking in the face of it. The scratching noise was right underneath her, and she looked down to see one of the old tree's branches swinging to and fro in the wind, scratching along the windowsill.

Shame burned in Tilly's belly. She pulled the window shut, her knees weak with spent fear and overwhelming relief, and she sank to the ground with her back to the wall. A burst of inexplicable tears coursed down her cheeks. She covered her face with her hands, weeping silently to avoid waking the children.

Just a branch. It had only been a branch. But it could have been Bert. He knew where they lived, he knew where they slept, he could find them, could come here into this cottage if he wanted to.

There would be no more sleep for Tilly tonight.

CHAPTER 6

TILLY SUPPOSED she shouldn't have been surprised by Robby's fever, but she still flinched when she laid a hand on his little forehead to find it burning with heat. His cheeks were very red, his eyes hollow as he looked up at her from his pillow. He kept grabbing at the covers, pulling them up to his chin.

"Robby, you're burning up," said Tilly softly, tugging the covers down a little way.

"I'm cold," Robby moaned. "Mama, I'm so cold."

It was the fever, Tilly knew, and she fought to hold back the rising frustration in her chest. She should have known that she'd been asking for this, dragging her three little children all over the city in the middle of winter, and yesterday had been especially brutal. It was a week before Christmas, with winter at its harshest, and the unrelenting wind had had all of them shivering when they had come home to nothing more than a bowl of watery soup to share between the three children. Tilly had skipped eating again yesterday, and now she wasn't sure if her headache was from exhaustion or sheer hunger.

"We're ready to go, Mama," said Janie from the doorway.

Tilly looked up at the child, who had somehow gotten herself and her three-year-old sister dressed and ready. Janie had deep circles under her eyes and a weary look to her, as though all the vibrancy of childhood had left her. Tilly tried to think of this, and not of the appalling reality that faced her: that she had to choose between scraping together some money for food and medicine or staying here and nursing her sick child. The thought of leaving Robby here all alone was brutal. But what else could Tilly do? She looked down at the boy, then up at the two girls, and as if on cue, Lissa gave a little moan and vomited on the bedroom floor.

"Lissy," cried Janie, grabbing her sister's shoulders.

"Oh, Lissa, my sweet child," gasped Tilly, rushing to Lissa's side. When she pushed the tiny girl's hair out of her face, she felt that Lissa, too, was burning with fever.

She certainly couldn't leave Lissa here alone. It was decided, then; Tilly had to stay here, but where would they find money? She had no idea.

"Come, Janie," she said, her voice quivering. "Let's put Lissa to bed, and then... then..." She stopped, not knowing what to say.

Janie's great, solemn eyes held hers. "I can beg, Mama."

Tilly stared at her. "What?"

"I can go on the corner of the street and beg," said Janie. "People give things to beggars. I'll ask nicely. And you could see me from the kitchen window."

Tears stung in Tilly's eyes. She knew that the little girl was right, right far beyond her years, that Janie's childhood had been stolen from her at the tender age of six. But the thought of her sweet little girl out on that street corner, subjecting herself to the shouts and spitting of a contemptuous crowd, was almost more than she could bear.

Yet what choice did she have? Robby was moaning in pain on the bed; Lissa was staring up at her with dull and listless eyes. They needed food and medicine, or...

Tilly's heart shrivelled at the terrible possibility. She couldn't contemplate that. These children were everything that she had, everything that she had left in the world to love.

She fought down her tears. "That's a good idea, my darling," she said softly. "Let's do that."

TILLY HAD no milk or coffee left for the sick children; only a tiny bit of herbal tea that a pitying neighbour had given her. It was just enough to turn the hot water into a tepid, yellowish fluid, but she told the children that it would do them good and managed to get each of them to drink a little. Lissa cried for hours, a shrill, steady whine that bore through Tilly's head. Robby was frighteningly quiet. He didn't sleep, just lay in bed shivering, his eyes vacant.

She spent the morning caring for her sick children, struggling with her fear and her helpless anger, and running to the kitchen window every few minutes to see if Janie was still all right on the street corner. The sight of her little girl on that corner was unbearable. Janie's face was dirty, her little dress torn; her filthy hair hung in bedraggled locks around her face. She was holding out her tiny hands, cupped, to every person that walked past, her face fixed in mute appeal. The appeal went unnoticed all too often.

Tilly agonized over what she would do if Janie didn't return with money. Leave her here in charge of her sick siblings while she went out seeking mending or laundry to do for someone? But Janie was much too young, and besides, she couldn't leave the children alone again, not after what had happened the last time. Then what? They needed medicine. Robby was shuddering with fever.

She could think of only one person who would help her, with Ray dead and Polly gone away for Christmas. Bert Carter. She knew that she only had to say the word, and he would give her children everything they wanted – food, medicine, an education. The thought of doing what he wanted, however, chilled her to the very bones. But what was worse? Losing herself, or losing them?

It was after noon when Lissa's wails finally subsided to quiet breaths as she drifted off to sleep. The lukewarm bath that Tilly had given Robby seemed to work a little, and he soon followed his sister into dreamland. Blissful silence settled upon the house. Tilly wanted to lie down and sleep right beside them, but she needed to check on Janie again. Tiptoeing across the room, she held her breath for every step she took before slowly pulling the door closed. Somehow, it didn't creak, and the children were sound asleep as she closed the door.

She let out a small breath of relief, and then a shout went up from the street. It was a pure, powerful, bright voice that she might have found beautiful on any other moment but this one.

"Pots and pans," it sang out. "The best cast-iron, lasts for generations. Get your pots and pans for Christmas. Wonderful gifts for the woman in your life."

"No," Tilly gasped, appalled. This hawker was going to wake her children, and she was so desperate for them to have a few moments of peace. Rushing through the house, she barged through the front door and saw him standing with his back to her, right in front of her house. There was a handcart beside him, all hung with pokers and grates and pots and pans of gleaming, dark iron, and he was holding up a huge cast-iron pot over his head. Muscles rippled in his shoulders, straining against his thin dark coat, as he called out.

"Look at this one. Perfect for a winter's stew," he called. "Easiest way to roast your Christmas goose."

"Sir. Sir!" Tilly gasped, rushing up to him. "Please – be quiet."

The man turned, lowering his pot, and Tilly was instantly struck by the colour of his eyes. They were the darkest brown she had ever seen and sparkled as though filled with stars, set beneath a head of tight black curls. She braced herself for his anger, but the corners of those eyes lifted as he gave her an uncertain smile.

"Excuse me, ma'am?" he said.

It had been such a long time since anyone had called her *ma'am*. She had been *ma'am* when Ray was still alive, when she still mattered. But as a penniless widow, she had simply been *you,* or *wretch*, or worse.

"Sir, please, I don't want to meddle with your business." Tilly fought back tears of desperation. "But I need some quiet. Please, just move along and cry your wares down the street. I have no money, and my neighbour is away. It'll do you no good to try to sell them here, in any case."

She took a step back, half expecting a blow or a spit in her direction. To her utter shock, the ironsmith's eyes widened, filling with softness.

"Oh, I'm sorry, ma'am," he said. "I didn't mean to give you any trouble, nor to disturb you."

Tilly blinked. She couldn't believe it. Everyone she met was resisting her somehow, but this man was hastily putting his pots and pans back into the handcart as if hasty to get out of her way. She knew she should get back inside to the children, but she had tasted a tiny bit of civility – if not real kindness – and she suddenly didn't want to let it go.

"Oh – it's all right," she said hastily, reaching out a hand as if to stop him, then tucking it under her arm instead as she hugged herself in the cold wind. "I'm sorry to come off so brusque. My children are ill, you see, and I've just gotten them to bed. They lost their father just a few weeks ago, and... I... I can't get them to a doctor."

The ironsmith paused, turning back to her. "I'm sorry to hear that, ma'am."

Tilly didn't know why she was telling him any of this. It wasn't his business, but it just poured out of her.

"They're so little," she said. "I had them out in the terrible cold yesterday, and I know it's my fault, it's... it's so hard." She bit back a sob.

"The cold is dreadful, ma'am," said the ironsmith, smoothly and without judgment. "How many do you have?"

"Three." Tilly half laughed, wiping at a tear. "Two girls and a boy."

"Ah, how lovely." The ironsmith grinned. "I can't wait to have children of my own someday. They are such delightful little things. Why, look at that sweet creature on the street corner." He gestured at Janie. "She has such wonderful manners."

"That's my eldest," said Tilly, deep shame opening a pit in her belly.

The ironsmith studied her for a moment, his head to one side. She saw something in his eyes that she couldn't quite read. Pity? No, not quite. Compassion? Tilly thought she may have forgotten what that even looked like.

"I'm Micah Conolly," he said suddenly, holding out a big, brown hand to her.

"Tilly Barton." Tilly shook it, hardly knowing why.

"I hope I haven't woken your children, Mrs. Barton," said Micah. "And I'll be praying that they get better soon." Something about the way he said it made Tilly believe it was actually true.

"Thank you," said Tilly. "And... Micah..."

He paused, halfway through lifting his handcart and going on his way. "Yes?"

"I appreciate your kindness," said Tilly. "Maybe more than you know."

He flashed her a smile that seemed to go right through her in a beam of jolting light. "See you around, Mrs. Barton," he said, as he lifted his handcart, and was gone.

CHAPTER 7

"Please, Lissa." Tilly felt she was choking on her tears as she scraped up a spoonful of the gruel and held it to her little girl's lips. She couldn't let Lissa see her crying with worry, but the gruel was going cold, and she only had one or two bits of coal left to burn during the night. "Just take a bite. You need your strength."

"Uh-uh." Lissa moaned. "Not hungry."

Those words struck a terrible chill into the pit of Tilly's stomach. She hadn't heard any of her children say them in such a long time.

"You'll feel better if you eat something," Tilly pleaded.

Robby moaned, his head tossing on the pillow, his little limbs jerking as a fever dream seized him. Janie was sponging his limbs with lukewarm water, her head nodding over her work. Midnight had come and gone, and the poor child had had no sleep tonight. She sat on the edge of the bed, mumbling reassurances to Robby, her small hands working constantly to cool him.

"What's wrong with Robby?" Lissa asked, her little voice stumbling over the words. A shudder ran through her. She, too, was running a dreadful fever.

"I'll tell you if you take one small bite," Tilly lied. She was growing desperate.

Lissa reluctantly nibbled a tiny bit of the gruel from the spoon, made a face, and swallowed it down. "What's wrong with him?" she asked shrilly.

"He's sick like you," said Tilly. "And you won't get better unless you eat another bite." She offered the spoon.

"Uh-UH." Lissa's voice rose to a shriek. She slapped at Tilly's hands, sending the spoon flying onto the floor.

"Lissa!" Tilly groaned, unable to keep the sharp surprise out of her voice. The spoonful of gruel splattered uselessly on the floor; the sight of such waste made her heart falter in her chest. She had only had a spoonful of this gruel to eat herself.

"Mama," moaned Robby, his limbs flopping as a long shudder wracked his body.

"I'll eat it, Mama," said Janie, her voice very faint. She turned an ashen face up to Tilly. "If Lissa doesn't want any."

"Don't WANT," howled Lissa, and launched into that wailing cry again.

Tilly handed the bowl to Janie, who dropped the sponge instantly and started inhaling the food in huge, starving bites. Tilly couldn't watch, couldn't bear to think of the poor child's hunger. She turned to Lissa instead, cradling the little girl in her arms, trying to hush her, but Lissa's cries only intensified.

"Come on, Lissy, come on," Tilly moaned, almost pleading with the child to stop crying. She closed her eyes tightly, bouncing Lissa gently in her arms. It had been so foolish to spend the few coins Janie had gotten on food instead of medicine. Why would the children eat if they weren't getting any better?

"Mama!" Janie let out a yelp of horror. "There's something wrong with Robby."

Tilly opened her eyes, and the sight she beheld gripped her heart with wrenching terror. Robby's limbs had sprung tight in an awful spasm, his head straining back against the pillow, his eyes rolling back white in his head. Janie gave a piercing shriek of terror, and then Robby's limbs started to jerk helplessly, a choking noise coming from his throat, foam flecking his tiny lips.

Tilly's body burned with terror. "Robby," she cried, putting Lissa quickly onto the bed. She scrambled over the bed, grabbing the little boy's tiny body. "Robby. Robby. Robby."

He sounded like he was choking; he didn't respond to her voice, his limbs flapping involuntarily. Tilly could only think to turn him on his side, slapping his back as though she could dislodge this terrible convulsion somehow.

"Robby!" she howled. Lissa and Janie were screaming in hysteria; Tilly wanted to scream too, wanted to grab the soul that seemed to be leaving her son's body and stuff it back inside him.

After a few seconds of absolute fear, Robby suddenly went limp. For a horrifying moment, Tilly thought the worst. Then his limbs twitched, and he turned his head, looking up at Tilly, his eyes very vague.

"Papa?" he whispered.

"No, baby, it's Mama." Tilly pulled him to her chest, holding him close, her limbs shaking uncontrollably. He looked at her with uncomprehending eyes, saliva sliding down his cheek. She wiped it away, cuddling him, inexpressibly relieved that he was awake, but terrified by his confusion.

He was sicker than she had thought, and she had nothing for him. She'd sold everything in their cottage to buy food: all the cutlery and crockery except what they absolutely needed, the furniture that Ray had chosen for them, the carpets, all their clothes but what they were wearing right now. Nothing was left. She had taken the very curtains from the bedroom, even though choosing them and putting them up was one of her favorite newlywed memories.

Now she had no way to find medicine for her children, and she knew, with a terrifying certainty, that Robby might not even make it through the night.

Lissa was still crying. Her constant wail sliced through Tilly's tired head, making it harder and harder to think. What could she do? To whom could she go? Polly had nothing, and she would only be back after New Year's.

The answer was obvious. Bert Carter.

Everything within her quailed, but now that she was staring at the spectre of death itself, even the thought of giving herself over to Bert paled in comparison to this unthinkable suffering.

"Mama," said Janie weakly.

Tilly looked up. Janie's cheeks were very flushed. "I... I feel dizzy," she croaked out, then gave a deep, hacking cough that bubbled ominously in her chest.

Tilly scooped Janie into her arms, alongside Robby and Lissa. She clutched them tightly, burying her face in their filthy hair, feeling the rattle of their sickly breathing. These children were everything. She would do anything for them.

Anything at all.

"It's all right, babies," she whispered. "It's going to be all right. Mama will make everything right, I promise."

It was then that she decided her own fate. Tomorrow morning, first thing, she would go to Bert Carter.

EVERY TIME RAY returned from a voyage, he had gifts for Tilly, expensive things that she didn't really need but always loved to have: paints and powders, perfumes and spices. Last time, he had brought her a tiny pot of the most beautiful rouge she had ever seen. It powdered one's cheeks with such a delicate blush of pink that it appeared utterly natural, and had a wonderful smell to it, too. She had worn it only on occasion, saving the last of it for the day that Ray was supposed to come home.

But Ray was never coming home. Tilly waited for the stab of grief as she sat down in front of her reflection in the kitchen window – she'd sold her mirror, too – and lifted the little metal pot to the light. But there was no grief; only a deadly resignation that made her sick to her stomach. She wasn't sure if she had come to terms with what she had to do or simply couldn't yet comprehend that she was actually doing it.

Taking a deep breath, Tilly started applying the rouge, hoping to ease away the black circles under her eyes and the hollow pallor of her cheeks. If this didn't work... She couldn't let herself think about that possibility. She untied her hair, loosening the mats with her fingers so that it fell down her back, plain brown, but it would have to do. It had done for Bert Carter before. She could only hope that he still wanted her now. The thought sent a horrible chill through her, like something cold and slimy slithering down her spine.

She spritzed her wrists with the tiny drop of perfume she had left, then tucked the empty pot and bottle carefully into the pocket of her dress – she would be able to sell them, she thought, if this didn't work – and took a deep breath. Robby and Lissa were whimpering in the bedroom; Tilly could hear Janie talking to them, her little voice broken by coughs.

Just a little longer, my babies, she thought, walking to the front door on wobbling knees. *Just a little longer, then everything will be all right.* She blinked back a tear, desperate not to ruin her rouge, and opened the front door.

For a jolting instant, she thought it was Bert standing on the threshold, as though her thoughts had somehow summoned him. When she leaped back with a gasp of shock and fright, though, she looked up into a pair of gentle brown eyes and a tender smile.

"M-Micah?" she stammered, instantly remembering the kindly ironsmith from the day before.

"Good morning, Mrs. Barton," said Micah. That beautiful smile turned a little shy. "You look very nice today, if you don't mind my saying so."

To Tilly's surprise, she didn't. There was something bashful and sweet about the way he said it; her guard rose at first, but she read no danger in his eyes.

"Thank you," she said. "That's a kind thing to say."

Micah blushed adorably. "I'm not here to bother you at all, I was just passing by, and..."

Tilly swallowed hard. She knew she had to fight down the temptation to stand here talking to Micah; she would linger here forever with him, she sensed, but she didn't have time. Her children didn't have time.

"I'm afraid I'm not buying any ironware today, Micah," she said, interrupting him as gently as she could.

"Ironware? Oh, no, ma'am, that's not why I'm here," said Micah.

A warning note sang out in Tilly's heart. She stepped back, a hand on the door. "Then what is it you want?" she asked shakily.

"Nothing – nothing. Please, ma'am, don't look so frightened," said Micah. "I – I just couldn't stop thinking about your poor little children, and how they need the doctor, and, well, I remembered that there's a clinic by the church open of a Tuesday, and the doctor doesn't charge a thing."

"I've heard of the clinic," said Tilly, exhaustion swamping her. "But it's all the way across the city. I could never get the children there. Even if I went myself, and begged for medicine, I couldn't get there and back in a day. I..."

"I know. I understand," said Micah gently. "My best friend is a cab driver, and he let me borrow his hansom cab for the morning, if we can get it back to him by twelve noon."

Tilly didn't understand what he was saying. She stared up at him for a few long seconds, her mind still occupied with getting away and going to Bert's offices.

"What?" she said, surprise and confusion turning her rude.

Micah blushed a little more. "I don't mean to pry, Tilly. You must think me terribly rude and nosy," he said. "I just... you... you seemed like you could use a little help. I hope I haven't offended you, and I ask your forgiveness if I did."

Tilly looked past him. A cab stood in the street, the horse waiting patiently. A cab.

"I can't drive," she said helplessly.

"I can," said Micah. "My master used to deliver ironware by cart, and I used to drive for him."

Tilly looked from the cab to Micah and back again, finally realizing what he was saying. He was taking the children to the clinic for her. He was helping her.

"Micah," she stammered out.

Little footsteps sounded on the kitchen floor. Janie's arms wrapped around Tilly's leg, and she leaned her little head against her mother.

"They won't stop crying," she whispered, her voice hoarse with sickness. "I can't get them to stop crying."

Tilly looked down at Janie, then up at Micah, her heart suddenly thundering with hope. She didn't have to go to Bert after all. There was another way.

Micah held out a hand to Janie, then gave Tilly a questioning look. "May I?" he asked.

"Yes." Tilly burst out. A gush of happy tears burst down her cheeks, washing away the rouge she no longer needed. "Yes, yes, please. I'll get the little ones."

"Wonderful." Micah grinned. "Let's go."

He scooped Janie into his arms and hurried to the cab, and Tilly turned and ran to the bedroom for Robby and Lissa, hardly believing that any of this was real and not just another fever dream.

CHAPTER 8

THE STREETS WERE WONDERFULLY cheerful on either side of the cab as it rattled toward home, the horse traveling at a merry clip, his knees thrown high, bells jingling brightly on his harness. Tilly hadn't ridden in a cab since the last time Ray was home, and she'd forgotten how much she liked it. Even the children were bright-eyed, pointing out the beauty of London's streets around Christmastime: the brightly decorated trees in the windows and on street corners, snowmen in back gardens hung with red scarves and silly hats, a huge painting of Father Christmas and his reindeer galloping across the large windows of a big clothing store.

Yesterday, the children would have been too sick even to notice the lovely decorations, no matter how much they liked them. Tilly was already overwhelmed with relief at the sight of their placid faces, but she kept reliving their visit with the doctor in her head.

"You have been lucky," he had told her, an elderly, grim-faced man with a long white moustache that drooped as he spoke. "If you had brought the little boy to me one day later, he would have no chance. The convulsion was as a result of the fever. You must keep them warm and dry, feed them as well as you can, and give them this medicine three times a day. And this one, twice a day."

There had been no charge for the medicine. Tilly had been so amazed at the thought of getting something without having to give anything in return that she had been too tongue-tied to thank the good doctor. Now, she thought, watching the children, they would be all right. The doctor had given them each something in a needle that had made them all scream except Janie, and it had worked very quickly. He had told her they would survive.

But if she hadn't brought them today... Tilly shivered. If Micah hadn't shown up at her door, would she have been able to bring them to any doctor today? Or would she still be at Bert's office, giving him all the "favors" he wanted until he would consent to saving her children?

The thought made her feel sick. She cuddled Lissa, who sat on her lap, and offered up a silent prayer of thanks for Micah, who was sitting up on the driver's seat while they rode in the nice, warm interior. She didn't know what she would have done without him.

She still wasn't sure that he wouldn't want something from her, either. But at least now her children were going to be all right. That had to be good enough for her right now, despite the tension growing in her belly.

Lissa was asleep on Tilly's lap, Robby's head was nodding, and Janie was yawning constantly by the time they got back to the cottage. Tilly stepped out of the cab with Lissa in her arms; Janie stumbled down beside her, clinging to her skirt.

"Thank you, Micah," she called up to him. "I'll just put Lissa in bed, then I'll get Robby and you can be on your way."

"It's still an hour before noon. Don't be rushed," said Micah, smiling. He climbed down from the driver's seat, carrying a nosebag in one hand, and hung it over the horse's ears. The animal chomped gratefully at its contents. "Can I bring Robby for you?"

That would mean Micah would come into the house, with the children all sleeping a drugged sleep after their medicine. Tilly's heart tightened with fear, but she didn't want to anger him.

"Yes, thank you," she stammered out through a dry mouth.

Micah lifted the sleeping Robby out of the cab, cradling the little boy easily in one arm as he closed the door. Robby's sleepy head lolled on his shoulder; the small hand came up, wrapped around Micah's neck and held on easily. Tilly was struck by an aching memory. When Robby was smaller, he had been plagued by nightmares, often running into their bedroom with tears in his eyes. He'd fall asleep between Tilly and Ray, and then Ray would carry him back to bed, with the little hand wrapped around his neck just as it was doing now with Micah.

She turned away, blinking back the painfully beautiful memory, and carried Lissa into the children's bedroom. Janie pulled back the covers and sat down; Tilly laid Lissa down, then started unlacing her shoes. Janie looked half-asleep already. Just as Tilly was pulling the covers over Lissa and bending to take off Janie's shoes, Micah came in with Robby, laying him gently on the pillow. He made no comment on the fact that there were no carpets or curtains in the house, nor any fire.

"Poor little mite," he said compassionately, pulling off the little boy's shoes.

"Mama, may I have some water?" asked Janie.

Micah was tucking the covers around Robby. "I'll bring her some," he said instantly.

"Oh – thank you," said Tilly, a little surprised. "In the kitchen."

Micah left, and Tilly let Janie climb into bed between her younger siblings. The little girl lay back on the pillow, looking up at Tilly with soft eyes. "Mama, who is that man?" she asked softly. "Is he an angel?"

"I don't know yet," said Tilly truthfully.

Micah returned with Janie's water, and the child drank thirstily before cuddling down between her siblings. And just like that, they were all three asleep: blissfully, silently, and peacefully asleep. Tilly allowed herself to breathe her first sigh of relief in what felt like a very long time.

But her relief was not yet complete. Micah led the way out of the room, and Tilly shut the door behind them both. She looked up at him, mute and suddenly frightened, waiting for him to say what he wanted, for the unwelcome touch, for the uncomfortable insinuation that she now owed him something.

Instead, Micah gave her a quick, gentle smile. "I hope they get much better now, Mrs. Barton," he said. "They're such beautiful children."

"Thank you," said Tilly. "So do I... they... they're my world."

"The doctor is a good man. He cared for me often when I was still on the streets," said Micah. "I know he'll have done his best to care for the children."

He stepped back, heading toward the kitchen, and that was when Tilly knew that he wanted nothing from her. Nothing at all. The relief was blessed, blissful, and it opened her eyes to just how dark and warm his eyes really were, just how open and friendly his smile.

"The streets?" Tilly echoed, sensing there was more to the story and suddenly wanting to know more about this gentle man who seemed to have a unique capacity to give without expecting anything in return.

Micah smiled, turning back to face her when she paused in the kitchen. "I don't remember my mother or father. The first thing I remember is being on the street with a gang of older boys who used to beg and steal to survive," he said. "I grew sick often then, and I'd go to that same clinic where the doctor would care for me. Eventually, he got me into an orphanage, and an ironsmith and his wife took me to be their apprentice from there when I was thirteen. His son had fallen in with the wrong crowd and become wayward, you see, so he taught me the trade instead." His voice softened. "The son still got the shop when he died and sold it to spend the money on all sorts of extravagances, but he could never take away my trade. I would still be on the street if it wasn't for the doctor and the ironsmith and the orphanage and so many other people who helped me."

"Well, I hope you know just how much you've helped us," said Tilly gently. "I... I would have had to do... something terrible." She stammered to a halt, shame boiling in her, wishing she hadn't said anything.

To her relief, Micah didn't ask. "I know there are many people in this city who aren't as lucky as I am. I might have to work out of my flat instead of a shop, but I have a roof over my head, and food, and a little money to put by for emergencies. I can't just turn away from those who are still struggling."

Tilly stared up at him in wonder. He truly was helping people because he just wanted to, she realized. They hadn't been the first ones either, she suspected, and was desperately grateful that Micah had come across their path when he did.

"Well, we're terribly, terribly grateful to you," said Tilly. "I'll repay you somehow, Micah."

"Don't say that." He held up a hand. "It's not necessary." His voice was tender but held firmness within it. "Now, I must take the cab back to my friend."

"Give him my thanks, too," said Tilly, wishing he didn't have to go. She hadn't realized how lonely she was until she'd started chatting with him.

"I will." Micah paused on the threshold, giving her another smile, dazzlingly white against the warm tones of his face. "I'll be back in this area again soon, I'm sure, and I'd love to stop by and see the children again if I may."

"Of course," said Tilly. "Of course."

She stood in the door and watched him drive away. Somewhere, a group of carollers was singing "O Come All Ye Faithful." It had just begun to snow, and in the house opposite hers, Tilly could see a young family decorating their Christmas tree together.

Perhaps Christmas was going to be all right, after all.

CHAPTER 9

As Tilly turned down the street to her cottage, part of her heart leaped, her eyes instantly scanning this way and that across the street in search of a tall figure hawking ironware with a handcart. It had only been a few days since she had last seen him, but every day she had woken with the hope that she might see him again soon.

Soon, perhaps, but not today. A note of disappointment ran through Tilly, her steps slowing as she walked toward her cottage. It was silly to be disappointed, she knew. Things were getting better; she had started to forget her fear of being followed, and to sleep better at night, too. Mrs. Plum, for whom she did the laundry, had given her an extra sixpence today for washing all her guests' laundry, too. It was enough that her children could have a square meal – and a hot one, too – on this Christmas Day: the pot in her arms contained some beef soup, and she even had a little bread at home to give them, if they hadn't already discovered and eaten it. This was a far cry from the treats Ray had always brought them at Christmas, the oranges and chocolate, the sweet white candy canes and toys, but it was something. They would be glad of it, and best of all, they were well enough to eat it.

She had very much to be thankful for right now, Tilly knew. She could forget, for today, the fact that another week had passed, and another week's rent was due. Bert would have paid it. Someday she would pay him back – in cold cash, so that she didn't owe him a thing. But for today, she would feed her children, and everything would be all right.

Tilly could hear them laughing as she pushed the front door open, and she paused in the bare kitchen for a few moments, her eyes closed, breathing in the glorious sound of their laughter. Then they came running in from the bedroom. Lissa still had a cough, but the others were all right, even if perhaps they had less bounce in their step than usual when they reached her.

"Mama. Mama," said Robby, his voice still a little raspy. "You're home."

"Mama." Lissa threw her arms around Tilly's legs and hugged them tightly.

Janie was hanging the kettle over the few coals that were left in the hearth from last night. She added two more from the coalscuttle, just enough to get the kettle to boil in a few minutes, and she turned her big eyes on her mother. "Can I help, Mama?" she said.

Tilly smiled down at them all. There were no gifts this Christmas, no bright decorations, no tree, but she still had most of her family, and she would be grateful for it today. "You can get out the breadknife, darling," she said. "We're having soup *and* bread today."

"Hooray," cheered Robby, throwing up his little fists.

Not so long ago, he would have complained about soup and bread. He far preferred pies and casseroles. Tilly tried not to think of that. She spooned out generous helpings of the soup for the children instead, cutting them thin slices of the bread, and tried not to mind that she couldn't have quite enough. Eating her bit of soup slowly, she tried to lose herself in the happy sight of the children gulping down their food. If it wasn't for Micah and the doctor, she knew, she might not be sitting here with them right now.

When the soft knock came at the door, Tilly's heart leaped at once. *Micah*. Maybe he had come to see them on this Christmas Day, after having been busy all week. She flashed the children an excited smile. "I'll be right back," she said, as she hurried to her feet, and answered the door.

"Merry..." She faltered. "Christmas."

It wasn't Micah. It was Mr. Jones standing on her step for the first time in weeks, and he was wearing a grim expression, his usual cheerfulness replaced by a terrible chill in his eyes.

"Good morning, Mrs. Barton," he said.

"Mr. Jones." Tilly swallowed hard, not knowing what to fear the most; that Bert had paid her rent, or that he hadn't. "Would you like some... some tea?" she said faintly. She thought there were still a few leaves left in the tin.

"I'm afraid not," said Mr. Jones. "Can you read?"

His brusqueness surprised her. Her heart had turned very cold in her chest. "Yes, sir," she said.

Mr. Jones held out an envelope. With a shaking hand, Tilly reached out to grasp it. He wouldn't let it go at first; she looked up, their eyes meeting, and another chill ran through her at the sight of his expression.

"I'm truly sorry about this, Matilda," he said. "You must understand that this isn't personal. I have expenses. A family of my own to think of. I have to put them first, even before you."

Before Tilly could say anything more, Mr. Jones let go of the envelope and strode away down the street.

"Mama?" called Janie from the kitchen table. "Who was that?"

Tilly forced her voice to be calm. "N-no one, my love," she called out. "I just need a little air."

She closed the door behind her and sank down onto the threshold, not caring that she was sitting in the cold snow. It was a beautiful day. A beautiful Christmas Day, except that she knew it was about to be ruined.

Slowly, she tore the envelope and took out the letter, and the word that grabbed her first told her everything she needed to know.

Eviction.

"Mama, I want home," said Lissa.

Her voice was very small, the words simple, but their poignancy wrenched at Tilly's heart. She clutched the child a little more tightly where she sat on Tilly's hip.

"This is going to be our home now, sweetheart," said Tilly shakily.

Lissa stared up mutely at the building in front of them. It was all that Tilly had been able to afford. She had found the listing in a newspaper that had come wrapped around a bit of fish she'd bought for the children; it had been very short, describing the places only as *Affordable rooms*. It had been the price that had caught Tilly's attention. She wasn't sure what "affordable" was when one couldn't afford anything, but the price was the cheapest she'd seen in a frantic week of searching for somewhere to go. She was well aware that Mr.

Jones only gave her until New Year's out of what faint kindness he could find for her in her heart. It turned out that after Bert's visit to their home, he had stopped paying their rent. Tilly had been relieved, at first, when the eviction notice had told her this. It meant that Bert was gone for good.

But their problems, she realized as she gazed up at the tenement building, were far from gone. A terrible feeling had risen in her stomach that they were only just beginning.

She had never seen a building so desolate. Perhaps a part of her had thought of herself and Ray as poor, because she had to be careful about their money, to sew all their own clothes, and couldn't wear nice jewellery or expensive perfumes. But now, as she clutched her children and shivered, she realized this was real poverty. There was hardly a windowpane in this building that still had any glass in it; the windows, instead, were covered up with cardboard or wood or fabric or simply left open to the wind that howled in a single, lonely note around the tall building. There were holes in the thin walls where the crumbling mortar had surrendered its grip to whole bricks. The door itself had been painted red once, but the ugly, bare wood shone through, splintered and neglected. But the worst part was the smell that sifted down from those open windows. Tilly couldn't quite describe all its nuances to herself, the combination of sourness and sickly sweetness, the strangely acrid reek beneath it all, but it chilled her.

"Mama, why do we have to live here?" asked Janie, looking up at Tilly with confusion in her eyes. "I like our house better."

They had all been born in that cottage. They didn't know any different.

"It's just for a little while, Janie," said Tilly.

Janie said nothing. Perhaps she sensed that Tilly was lying to herself.

"I'm hungry," said Robby. It was a listless little statement; he had grown used to saying it without any results.

There was nothing else for it. Tilly squared her shoulders, tightened her grip on Lissa's little body and Robby's little hand, and checked that Janie was holding her skirt.

"Whatever happens, my darlings," she said aloud, "always know that I love you."

Then she stepped forward into the appalling stench of her future.

PART II

CHAPTER 10

Two Years Later

TILLY'S black-and-white uniform was still as uncomfortably tight around her chest as it had been the day she first walked into the Hambrights' mansion eighteen months ago now. That was because their previous scullery-maid, who had had the good sense to die wearing her own clothes instead of her uniform, had been a girl of twelve; most scullery-maids were no older than that. Tilly, however, had no references. Scullery-maid was the best she could get.

She shrugged her shoulders, trying to shift the uncomfortable fabric just a little as she trudged down the street toward the tenement, her feet sucking and crunching in half-frozen mud. It was hard to believe they were approaching yet another

Christmas in the tenement, but the icy ground was irrefutable proof. She skirted around a pile of nameless filth, dodging a dead cat lying stiffly in the street. The long walk from the mansion to her tenement was only one of the disadvantages that a less desperate woman would have found unacceptable about her position with the Hambrights, she thought. But for her, it was an advantage: it meant she could still see her children every night. She would never have been allowed to bring them to the mansion.

And in winter, it was truly night by the time she reached the looming ugliness of their building. Avoiding the strange old man who slept on the street corner and tended to grab at one's skirts if he thought he had half a chance, Tilly dug out her rusty key and unlocked the front door of the building. It swung open with a long moan, and she paused in the darkness after shutting it, listening to the steady chaos of the other tenants at night. Someone was drunkenly singing a bad rendition of "I Saw Three Ships": *on Christmas day in the morning.* They slurred their words. Tilly thought of the picture-perfect little Hambright girls and the ribbons in their hair and their neatly enunciated version of the same song, and she ached with all her soul to see her own girls like that.

Instead, when she stumbled down the creaking steps to their tenement in the cellar, Tilly could barely see through the smoke that permeated every corner of the room. The cellar had been roughly divided into two rooms, both of which were roughly the size of the bedroom she'd had in the cottage. The old lady who lived in the other half of the cellar, Mrs. Gottun, always kept a fire going at this time of year. She argued that the smoke was better than the cold, and Tilly was too tired to do anything but agree with her.

She waved away some of the smoke before closing the door behind her and stepping into the dinginess of the room that was now her home. It contained very little: a poorly ventilated little hearth, a small wooden trunk containing the bits of kitchenware Tilly had scrounged over the years, and two sleeping pallets. There was only one washroom for the entire building, and it was up on the third floor. There was a small gas lamp burning on the wall, and the children were huddled beneath it, cuddling under a threadbare blanket. Their big, round eyes rested on Tilly, and smiles appeared instantly. With cries of "Mama. Mama!" they burst out from under the blanket and ran to her, throwing little arms around her legs.

"Oh, my darlings." Tilly sighed with relief, sinking to her knees and hugging them tightly. They were dirty, ragged young things now, but they were hers, and her thirteen-hour days were worth every minute just to come home to this.

"Matilda, you're late," barked a voice from the other side of the room.

Tilly raised her head. Mrs. Gottun's unpleasantly lumpy figure leaned against the wall at the corner of the room where the rickety wooden partition between their rooms ended in a gap.

"Lady Hambright had visitors today, Mrs. Gottun," said Tilly, as patiently as she could. She rose from the tangle of happy limbs and reached into her pocket, drawing out an entire shilling, one-fifth of her weekly wage. She handed it over to Mrs. Gottun; the old woman knew that she had no one else to watch the children during the day, and she certainly capitalized on it.

Mrs. Gottun pocketed the money without so much as saying *thank you*. "The child was a complete nuisance today," she snapped. "You should really teach her some manners."

"I'm sorry, Mrs. Gottun," said Tilly, gritting her teeth. "I'll certainly have a word with her."

She spotted a leering face looking around Mrs. Gottun's waist. It was the eldest of her three repulsive little sons, Percy, and Tilly had never met a child she hated, but Percy came close enough. He gave her a gap-toothed grin and thumbed his nose at her. Tilly managed a thin smile.

"Well, see that you do," grumbled Mrs. Gottun, "or my price will go up."

She turned and shuffled away, and Tilly returned to the children with a sigh. Lifting a canvas satchel down from her shoulder, she forced a smile for them. "Who's ready for dinner?"

The response was a chorus of clamouring, hungry little voices, and Tilly laughed despite herself, reaching into her bag for the bread-and-butter she'd prepared for them at work with the bread she'd bought that morning. The cook, who had a kind heart even though she tried to hide it, had given her a few scraps of fish at lunchtime too, and the children were soon eating contentedly.

"Did you have any luck today, my darlings?" Tilly asked, trying to keep her tone very light.

Janie raised her head, and Tilly was struck, as she often was, by her daughter's growing beauty. Somehow the long nose and dark hair that Tilly thought plain on herself were striking on Janie, with the promise of a timeless elegance to her features despite the fact that she was only eight years old.

There was something else about her tonight, though: her cheeks seemed more pinched than before, her eyes perhaps set a little deeper. Was Tilly imagining it, or had Janie grown even thinner? She must be growing taller.

"A little, Mama," said Janie softly. "A bob in total; a tanner and a thruppence for me, and three pennies for Robby."

"That's good. That's very good," said Tilly, who had hoped for more. She reached for the newspaper she'd stolen from a rubbish heap earlier that week. "Who's ready for some reading?"

"I am," said Janie instantly. Robby groaned, and Lissa sighed. "I'm tired, Mama." she announced.

"I know, darling," said Tilly. "But if you get an education, then you might be able to improve your station in life someday."

"What does that mean?" moaned Lissa.

"Mama explains it every night," said Janie impatiently. "It means that one day you might have a better house and more money, but you'll have to pay more attention – both of you."

Lissa stuck out her tongue at her sister, but Janie didn't see, and Tilly was too tired to do anything but let it slide. Truth be told, she was too tired for these lessons herself, but she couldn't bear the thought of her daughters someday being as helpless as she'd found herself when Ray died. Someday, she would get them into school, and then they could become nurses or clerks or anything except dirt poor.

She lifted the paper, scanning down to the place where she'd left off the night before. "All right," she said. "Pay attention now. I'm going to read the paragraph first, and then Janie will read a bit, then Robby, then Lissa."

"We always do it that way, Mama," said Robby, with barely disguised frustration.

Tilly ignored him. "*TENSIONS RISING IN TRANSVAAL*," she read. "*The Boers of Transvaal in Southern Africa have been seeking independence...*"

When she reached the end of the paragraph, she looked up, eager for Janie to read the headline and learn all the exotic words and phrases in the article. But she was met with a disappointing, yet charming sight. Janie was lying on the ground, her head pillowed on her arm; Robby lay with an arm around his sister, and Lissa lay hugging Robby's legs, her head on his hip. They were all fast asleep.

Tilly sighed. She should wake them and make them continue their education. She firmly believed that it was their only hope. Instead, she picked them up and carried them, one by one, to their sleeping pallets. Then she curled herself around Lissa, pulled a thin blanket over her shoulders, and told herself that tomorrow would be better.

She had been telling herself this for what seemed like a very long time.

❦

TILLY SQUINTED down at the pot in her hands, scouring at a suspicious spot on the bottom. The Hambright mansion was an elderly one: the family had been wealthy for many generations, and some of the things in this house were so old Tilly couldn't even guess at their age. She suspected this pot was one of them.

Stifling a yawn, Tilly gave the bottom of the pot another scrub with the rag. She was so close to finishing the supper dishes, and when she was done with washing and rinsing them, she still had to dry them, put them away, sweep out the scullery, and set out the fire for the morning. It was nine o' clock at night already, and Tilly doubted she would reach home before eleven.

Still, something about this pot worried her. She plunged it to the bottom of the soapy water, then raised it, squinting at the bottom. It was as she suspected: the pot was leaking, a tiny trickle of water dripping out from underneath.

Telling the cook would take only a few minutes, yet Tilly was deeply tempted to just forget about it until tomorrow morning. But Mrs. Scott would want this pot for tomorrow morning's porridge. Sighing, Tilly rinsed the pot, dried it, and trooped into the kitchen with it in her arms.

"Mrs. Scott?" she said. "I think this pot has a hole in it."

Mrs. Scott looked over from where she was kneading tomorrow morning's bread. "Are you sure, girl?" she barked.

"I believe so, ma'am," said Tilly. "It seemed to be leaking when I was washing it. Perhaps I'm imagining things."

"No, no," said Mrs. Scott, with her gruff kindness. She took the pot from Tilly, holding it up to the light. "Why, it's but a pinprick, yet you're right, girl," she said.

Tilly refrained from pointing out that she was near enough to Mrs. Scott's own age. "What shall I do with it, ma'am?"

"Just set it aside," said Mrs. Scott. "The housekeeper next door was just mentioning to me that she has a good tradesman for this kind of thing coming to her house tomorrow; I'll send you over there tomorrow morning to have it mended, or replaced, whichever he thinks best."

"Thank you, ma'am," said Tilly, feeling a faint flutter of excitement. Any day that wasn't spent washing dishes from morning till night was at least a nice little change for her, and those days were rare enough.

She plodded home, only reaching the building at a quarter past eleven with food for the children. There were jacket potatoes tonight, as well as some stew, and Tilly was hoping that the stew would be enough for now so that the children would have something to eat tomorrow. Stumbling down into the cellar, she realized that she had stumbled upon bath time – or at least, the sad parody of bath time that they had in this, their new life. Back in the cottage, their weekly bath time had been hard work but always a time of hilarity; Tilly would heat the water on the hearth and fill the tin tub in the washroom, then scrub the children one by one, starting with Janie. Shoving Robby and Lissa into the tub at the same time was always the easiest, but wrangling the slippery, soapy toddlers had always been a little chaotic.

Now, Janie was sitting in front of the fire, shivering as she wiped at her body with a rag she'd dampened in the bucket of cold water beside her. Her back was to the door, and Tilly felt a jolt of utter shock run through her as she looked at her little girl. Janie had always been a skinny child, even more so since Ray had died. But this... She had never seen Janie looking like this. She could see every bone in her child's spine, every rib with great hollows beneath them, the tiny waist cruelly nipped in beneath the ribcage, the bones of the pelvis straining against the skin. Janie dried herself with a bit of old sackcloth, then pulled her faded dress over her head.

"Mama's home," cried Lissa, bouncing up out of her sleeping pallet.

The children swarmed around her, and Tilly hugged and kissed them, trying not to let on how shaken she was. She needed to talk to Janie, to find out what was happening and why her daughter was so desperately thin when they were eating every night now that she worked for the Hambrights. To Robby's and Lissa's delight, Tilly put them straight to bed after supper, and then sat down with Janie in front of the hearth.

"Why aren't Lissa and Robby reading with us tonight, Mama?" Janie asked, her eyes wide as though she feared Tilly had given up on the two little ones.

Tilly didn't want to frighten her. "I just thought it would be nice to spend some time together, just the two of us," she said, forcing a smile. "Now, tell me — do you think you can read this paragraph on your own, without me starting you off?"

"Oh. Yes, I can, Mama, please — let me try," said Janie, her eyes lighting up. "Let me try." She eagerly took the paper from Tilly and began to read, a little haltingly, but almost flawlessly. *"BIRMINGHAM PRIEST IMPRISONED UNDER PUBLIC WORSHIP ACT..."*

Tilly listened, her heart filled with mingled terror and pride. She saw so much in Janie, so much of Ray's fearless determination, and a quiet strength that was all her own. The thought that it could all be snuffed out by whatever cruel illness had stolen the meat from her bones – it was unbearable.

"That was beautiful, my darling," said Tilly softly.

"Thank you, Mama." Janie gave her a bright smile. She seemed cheery enough; Tilly saw no rash, no cough, no signs of a fever.

She returned the smile, striving to hide her worry, then reached over and laid a hand over Janie's. "My darling," she said, "I'm going to ask you something, and I want you to answer me honestly, do you understand?"

Janie's eyes widened. "Yes, Mama?"

"Do you have any aches or pains?" Tilly asked her gently. "Anything I should know about?" She squeezed Janie's hand lightly, fighting to keep the quiver from her voice. "You've become dreadfully thin, my dear."

Janie dropped her eyes to the ground immediately. "No, Mama," she said, a little too quickly.

Janie never lied, but Tilly knew that she was lying now, and it made her heart stutter in her chest. So it was true: Janie was sick, and she had been hiding the truth from Tilly in a bid to protect her.

"Janie, I'm not angry with you." Tilly struggled to control her voice. "But you must tell me the truth right away. If you are sick, my darling, then there are things we can do. We can go back to the clinic that treated you two Christmases ago. But we have to do it now, before..." Tilly couldn't go on. Her voice cracked, and she fell silent to protect her daughter from the terrible nearness of her tears.

"I'm not sick, Mama." Janie raised her eyes, and they were pleading, but genuine. "I promise I'm not sick. I would tell you if I was."

Tilly searched Janie's eyes, perplexed. "But then why are you so thin?" she asked. "It makes no sense, Janie. Even if you don't have any pain or rash or any such thing, I'll have to take you to the doctor. You're not well."

"I'm not sick," Janie repeated. "I know it for sure." She dropped her eyes again, her cheeks colouring. "I... I know why I've gotten a little thin."

"A little thin. Janie, you're emaciated."

"I'm sorry." Without warning, Janie burst into tears, clapping both hands over her face. "I didn't want you to know. You're not meant to know. They'll – they'll throw us out."

Tilly had never been so frightened. She grasped Janie's wrists, pulling her hands away from her face. "Tell me," she said, her voice openly shaking now. "Tell me what's happening to you."

Sniffling, tears gushing down her cheeks, Janie raised her face. "The − the food you leave for us, Mama," she stammered out. "I've been giving all of mine to Percy."

Tilly stared at her, not sure whether to be relieved or shocked by the simple yet confusing explanation. "Why would you do that, Janie?" she asked. "The Gottuns are far better off than we are, considering Mr. Gottun has work, and I pay Mrs. Gottun to care for all of you."

"He wouldn't stop. He said he'd take Robby's and Lissa's if I didn't give him mine," Janie snivelled. "And he pulled my hair and pushed me and made Lissa cry. I hate it when Lissa cries." She wept. "I'm sorry, Mama, I'm so sorry."

"Oh, Janie..." Tilly reached for the child, pulling her into her arms. "Janie, Janie, my sweetheart, why didn't you tell me?"

"Percy said he would get us all thrown out," sobbed Janie. "And then where would we go?"

Tilly hugged Janie tightly, saying nothing. She knew full well that the Gottuns were long-term tenants who had always managed to be on the good side of their cold and heartless land-lord, Mr. Finch, and she had no doubt that Percy would indeed be able to persuade Mrs. Gottun to get the Bartons thrown out.

But the thought of that rude little child stealing from her Janie – and stealing for weeks or months or even more, judging by how unbelievably thin Janie had become – made something dark and bitter boil in her gut. She worked so hard for every shred of food she could give her children. The thought of having that taken right from Janie's mouth was sickening.

"All right. All right," said Tilly soothingly as Janie's sobs subsided. "It's going to be all right, Janie. I want you to go to bed now, and I'll deal with Percy."

"But Mama, what if..." Janie began.

"No what-ifs for you, little lady," said Tilly firmly. She kissed Janie on the forehead. "I forbid it. You're to forget all about this now, and leave it to me, do you understand?"

Janie's little shoulders slumped with relief. "All right, Mama," she said, childlike faith evident in her voice.

"Good girl. Now go to bed."

Janie obediently went and tucked herself into the sleeping pallet beside Robby. Tilly knew that she would be asleep in seconds, exhausted by an endless day of caring for her younger siblings. If Percy was stealing Janie's food, Tilly wondered, was Mrs. Gottun keeping even half an eye on the children? Tilly gave her a whole shilling each week to do so, and the thought that that money was being wasted enraged her. She stood up, dusting off her skirt, and marched over to the gap in the wall.

It was well past midnight by now, and Tilly had to leave for work again at five. But she couldn't care less, not at this moment; nor did she care that the Gottuns may be sleeping.

"Mrs. Gottun," she shouted into the dinginess of their room.

It appeared that the old lady was still awake for some reason. She came up to the gap in the wall, her rheumy eyes scanning quickly over Tilly with growing distaste.

"What do you want?" she demanded. "I'm not going to care for your brats on a Sunday afternoon, too, if that's what you wanted to ask me. I know full well that you have that time off, but you can look after your own brood then, and be a mother for once."

Tilly felt a wave of blind fury engulf her at Mrs. Gottun's cruel words, perhaps because she feared that they might be true; that she had taken so many weeks to discover her daughter wasn't eating, to realize the food was being stolen right from her mouth.

"It's nothing like that, Mrs. Gottun," said Tilly sharply, barely controlling her rage. "This is about Percy."

Mrs. Gottun raised a lazy eyebrow. "Percy?"

"Yes, your son." Tilly folded her arms. "I pay you a shilling each week to care for my children, but instead, I have just found out that your own son takes my children's food when you are meant to be caring for them."

Mrs. Gottun's eyes narrowed, and Tilly knew but did not care that she was treading on thin ice. "That shilling is a pittance, and you know it," she snarled.

"A pittance, perhaps, for work done," Tilly spat, "but not for what you're doing, which is nothing – or, worse, stealing from my own children. Your son is a thief."

"How dare you," Mrs. Gottun gasped, clapping a hand to her chest. "How could you?"

"On the contrary, Mrs. Gottun, how could *you* allow it?" shouted Tilly. "You're letting my children starve."

Mrs. Gottun's cheeks were scarlet with rage. "This has nothing to do with me," she shouted.

"No, it doesn't – not anymore," spat Tilly. "You will never set foot in my rooms again, and I don't want you anywhere near my children." She planted her hands on her hips. "I'll pay you this week's shilling, and that will be the last of it. Janie can take better care of her siblings than you ever could – and I suspect she's been doing this all along, anyway."

Mrs. Gottun's eyes flashed then, and Tilly knew that she had made the old woman angry. Mrs. Gottun took a step toward her, pointing a threatening finger under her nose.

"You don't want to do this," she hissed. "You don't want to take that money from me."

Tilly looked into her eyes, and her resolve wavered for an instant. What if Mrs. Gottun went to Mr. Finch, and got Tilly and the children thrown out? Would Tilly come home next Monday night to find that her children were huddling on the frozen streets outside instead of in the comparative shelter of their pitiful tenement?

But Tilly couldn't care about any of that. Not after what had happened to her poor, dear Janie.

"I already have, Mrs. Gottun," she spat. "Now leave my children alone. They will have instructions not to allow you or your awful little boy into our rooms, ever again."

She swept away, her anger fizzling out and giving way to a desperate fear. It would be good to save that shilling each week, that much was certain.

But if Mrs. Gottun had them evicted from their tenement... Janie's question rang painfully in Tilly's mind as she climbed onto the pallet beside Lissa and wrapped her arms around the child's tiny, sleeping figure. *And then where would we go?*

CHAPTER 11

THERE WAS no darkness like the utter black hours before dawn in the middle of a winter's night. There were street lamps along most of the route to the Hambright mansion once Tilly had left the slums proper behind, but the watery circles of pale-yellow light they cast seemed to do little more than be mocked by the darkness. Tilly's skin always crawled as she made short dashes from street lamp to street lamp, hating the pitch dark, the yawning alleys, the black doorways.

At least she had almost reached the mansion now, but that also meant there were fewer street lamps along the roads between manor grounds, and Tilly had to rely on the bright gas lights on the manor gates instead. She jogged in the dark stretches in between, always feeling like something was nipping at her heels.

It was silliness, Tilly knew. There was nothing following her. In fact, at this hour, there was no one outside on the streets at all; she hardly ever met a soul on her journey to work, except for one stretch through the slum where factory workers were stumbling off to another day of perilous toil.

She forced herself to slow down a little, saving her energy for the long day ahead even though this was the stretch she hated the most. It was a great, yawning black gap between the Hambrights and their neighbors, both of whom had vast grounds with hardly any lights at all except those that shone around the mansions themselves where they stood proudly surrounded by stretches of green lawn. Tilly could see nothing in the darkness except for the golden promise of the lights in the Hambright mansion; there were lights outside the door, and a few on in the washrooms upstairs, and of course in the kitchen below. She kept her eyes fixed on the square of light from the kitchen window. There was no sound at all save for the crunch of snow beneath her feet.

Or was there?

Tilly froze. She could swear she had heard something behind her. Something that sounded like footsteps.

Bert Carter swam into Tilly's mind, unwelcome as always, yet somehow always finding his way into her thoughts even though she had been rid of him for a full two years. She whirled around, her eyes probing the darkness, remembering the way his hands had felt on her, the way he had leered at her, and her heart was hammering in her throat. Would anyone hear her scream out here?

"H-hello?" she stammered into the impenetrable blackness.

There was no response. Then, a crunching – something on the snow. Tilly cringed, whirling to face it, but it was heading away from her, up the grounds belonging to the Hambrights' neighbors.

A fox, she told her hammering heart. It had to be a fox. It was foolish to fear Bert, all this time later, when she knew he had forgotten about her long ago. If only she could forget about him half as easily.

She shook herself, wrapping her arms more tightly around her waist, and hurried on toward the Hambright mansion.

"TILLY!" shouted Mrs. Scott.

Tilly was, at that moment, on her hands and knees scrubbing out the last corner of the scullery. It was a large room, and she had been scrubbing for hours; it was a relief to get up. She stretched her back, ignoring the aches in her joints, as she walked into the kitchen.

"Yes, ma'am?" she asked, blinking back her exhaustion. She had struggled to sleep after her confrontation with Mrs. Gottun yesterday, and now she was feeling it.

"My friend from next door just sent a pageboy over to let me know that the man with the ironware has arrived. He's busy and won't have time to stop by here, but if you run over there with the pot you can get his opinion." Mrs. Scott handed Tilly the pot. "I'll arrange with my friend for payment if he wants to mend or replace it. Hurry now – lunch dishes will be arriving soon."

"Yes, ma'am. Thank you, ma'am," said Tilly, taking the pot in her arms.

It was an unusually pleasant winter's day that Tilly stepped into. The snowfall was light enough that walking across the grass was easy, and the sun was shining for once, even if the breeze was cold and small clouds kept scudding over its bright face. Still, it was good – if strange – to feel real sunlight on her face for once. In winter it felt as though the sun became something distant to her, something she barely knew existed.

Hugging the pot to her chest, Tilly tried to relax a little, moving her shoulders to work some of the kinks out of them. She wondered if Mrs. Gottun was going to get them evicted after all. She wondered if Janie had really eaten her breakfast today. If they were evicted, where would they go? Perhaps she could persuade Mrs. Scott to give them a room in the servants' quarters. Tilly could make do with a narrow bed and a tiny room with three children in it; she'd sleep on the floor if she had to. It would be better than the streets.

Surely, anything would be better than the streets.

The Fanning mansion was almost as big and imposing as the Hambrights', with vast gardens that were bright and extravagant in the spring. Now, they slumbered beneath a blanket of pure white snow, but that had not prevented the Fannings from expressing their wealth in other ways. Even though there were still weeks to go before Christmas, the Fannings had already started on their decorations. Strings of bunting hung in the pine trees bordering the drive; when Tilly approached the servants' entrance, she saw there was already a wreath on the door.

There was a donkey standing in the stable yard by the servants' entrance, harnessed to a tiny cart that was hung with all sorts of ironware. It flicked its ears toward Tilly as she approached, and its nose was so velvety she couldn't resist taking one hand off the pot and reaching toward the soft, white nose. As she did so, a huge brown hand appeared out of nowhere and seized her wrist, stopping her just as the donkey's ears suddenly flattened to its skull and a set of massive yellow teeth snapped shut mere inches from her fingers.

"Oooh," squealed Tilly in shock, yanking away her hand.

"I'm afraid you don't want to do that, ma'am," said a warm, friendly, and overwhelmingly familiar voice. "She looks friendly enough, but she doesn't like strangers."

That voice. It shot right through Tilly's heart and into one of her fondest memories: memories of a stranger's kindness, a kindness as unexpected as the happy tenderness in the voice speaking to her right now.

She turned around, not believing it until her eyes found his dear face, his warm smile, his crop of tight black curls.

"Micah?" she breathed.

Micah's eyes widened. "Tilly?" he said. "Can it be?"

"It is." Tilly began to laugh, tears suddenly filling her eyes at the same time. She didn't know where the laughter or the tears were coming from, but she knew she was delighted to see him. "It's been so long."

"Two years," said Micah. He stepped toward her, reached out a hand as though to touch her, then let it fall by his side. "Why, I've been wondering where you went. I was back at that cottage many times right after Christmas, but you were never there."

"You – you came back to the cottage?" asked Tilly, shocked.

"Of course. I was looking for you," said Micah. "I wanted to know about the children..." His voice trailed off. "How are the children?"

"They're fine. They're just fine," said Tilly, even though she knew it wasn't quite true. "They're getting so big," she added, hoping to cover the pang of guilt she felt at the thought of poor Janie.

"Oh, that's wonderful." Micah beamed. "I'm so happy to hear that. I think of them so often... and... and of you." A blush warmed his cheeks, and Tilly found it more appealing than she could say.

"You. Ironsmith!" barked a voice from the servants' entrance. "You're not being paid to stand around all day. This grate isn't going to repair itself."

The Fanning cook's voice jolted Tilly sharply back to her own harsh reality. She couldn't afford to be standing here chatting with Micah either, no matter how much she wanted to do so — more than anything in the world.

"I should go, too," she said. "Mrs. Scott is waiting for me." She held out the forgotten pot in her arms. "She asked if you could mend or replace this."

Micah took it, giving it a quick glance. "Oh, this is nothing. I'll be able to mend it. The cook here mentioned someone would be coming over from the Hambright mansion." He smiled at her. "I never dreamed that it would be you."

"I'm glad to see you again, Micah," said Tilly softly. "A page will be over for the pot later, with your money."

He hesitated. "Tilly... I... I would very much like to see you again, when it suits you," he said.

Tilly's heart flipped over. What was that in his eyes? Softness? Compassion? It wasn't pity; that much she knew. "The children would be delighted to see you again," she said.

"Are you living at the servants' quarters?" asked Micah.

"No... it's... in the slums." Tilly blushed.

"Where exactly?" asked Micah, not missing a beat.

She gave him her address. "I get a little time off on a Sunday afternoon," she said. "It would be good to see you... truly, it would."

Micah gave her a wide smile. "I'll see you all on Sunday," he said warmly.

Tilly wanted to stay here in this stable yard with him forever, but she knew she had to go before she angered Mrs. Scott. She backed away, the day suddenly looking brighter than before, the sky bluer, the clouds fluffier, the snow more sparkling. "See you Sunday," she echoed.

For the first time in many years, Tilly turned away with something to look forward to in her future. Maybe this would be the first Christmas since Ray died that things might look up for her and the children.

CHAPTER 12

FOR ONCE, despite the late hour and the bitter cold that reached around every corner to sting Tilly's nose and ears, she had a spring in her step as she walked home. Something about the few minutes she had spent talking to Micah earlier that day had filled her heart with warmth and light, as though a hearth fire had been started within her soul.

Earlier, when she had met Micah, Ray's death had still been so raw. But as the years had passed, Tilly's shock had given way to a kind of hollow resignation rather than wrenching grief. There were times, now, that Tilly wondered if she had ever really loved Ray, or if she had loved him only for what he had given her: the cottage, the children, her happy life with them. So this time, when she thought about the way everything inside her fluttered at the sight of Micah, there was nothing holding her back from that feeling.

And he wanted to see her on Sunday afternoon. Tilly had an extra bounce in her step at the very thought. She fell into a happy daydream as she pushed her way through the streets, busy with the flood of factory workers heading for home at the same late hour that she did. She imagined the knock at her tenement door, pushing it open, the happy squeals of the children when they saw Micah standing there. Even the way he said her name filled her with thrilling joy: *Tilly*. She could almost hear him now...

"Tilly."

Tilly stumbled to a halt, startled. Had that been part of her daydream, or had she just heard her name on the wind?

A sudden chill ran up her spine, the happy daydream falling to fragments around her feet. Someone in the crowd jostled her, making her stumble to the side. She whirled around, and for a dreadful instant, she thought she saw him – the strong frame, the thick black hair, the cold grey eyes – but then the half-glimpsed profile was lost in the crowd, and Tilly was left standing there, her heart shuddering her entire body with the force of its pounding.

"It's not him," she told herself out loud, wrapping her arms around herself against the cold. Of course, it wouldn't be. What would Bert be doing down here in these slummy streets? She was imagining things, as usual. She had to stop thinking Bert was following her when it had been two years since she'd even heard from him.

Turning around, Tilly let out a sigh and continued toward home, feeling her fears fade away in the face of her excitement. It was Friday today. Only two more days before she saw Micah again, and maybe then she would forget all about Bert Carter.

Maybe then she would be able to think of her future for once, instead of the lost, happy past and the desperate, hard present.

⚜

TILLY HAD BEEN abuzz ever since she got home from work that Sunday afternoon around half past twelve, and her nervous energy seemed to have reached the children, too. Even Robby was bouncing around the little tenement, chattering excitedly as Tilly made a hearty attempt at some form of tidying up.

"When is he coming, Mama? Can I hug him? Does he remember me?" Lissa clamoured, following Tilly this way and that as she tried to make the smelly, smoky little room a bit more presentable.

Tilly folded up one of their blankets and placed it at the feet of her pallet, trying to push down her shame at the fact that Micah would see this place. "Of course, he remembers you, Lissy," she said. "He asked about you."

"Shall I put the kettle on, Mama?" asked Janie sensibly.

"Oh – yes. Yes, we'll have to give him some tea. You do that, Janie," said Tilly. She felt as though she'd completely forgotten how to be a hostess at all. Glancing around the room, she saw that it was only moderately neat and not particularly clean and knew that there was nothing she could do about either reality. With a quivering fear in the pit of her stomach, she realized that she could only hope that Micah would be able to see past this.

Taking a few deep breaths, Tilly tried to steady herself. She was trying her best not to get ahead of herself, but she knew how Micah had looked at her, knew that he was calling on her about more than just the children, and knew that the chance existed – perhaps vanishingly small, but nonetheless present – that maybe one day he would marry her. The thought of having more than one income to help her raise the children, was almost as exciting as the thought of being married to a man as kind and handsome as Micah Connoly.

There was a soft tap at the tenement door, and Tilly whirled around. "It's him," she gasped, hurrying to the door.

For a second, when she reached the door, Tilly remembered the last time she had thought Micah had come to see her. She remembered the jolt she'd felt when she'd swung the door open to see Mr. Jones standing there instead, eviction notice in hand. But this time, when she opened the door, it was him: his soft eyes, his gentle smile, his warm voice saying, "Well, look how big you all are," as the children rushed at him with shouts of glee.

They assailed him with hugs, and Tilly watched in surprise. Ever since moving to the slums, she had cautioned her children against strangers, and they normally avoided and feared anyone they didn't know. But it was different with Micah.

He looked up at her from amid the tangle of hugging limbs around him, and he was beaming, his eyes filled with joy.

Maybe everything was going to be different with Micah, Tilly thought.

TILLY COULD HARDLY BELIEVE JUST how much easier the donkey cart had made her life. Even though Magi, the donkey, was not particularly fast, her little hooves nonetheless made much quicker progress through the winding streets than Tilly's own feet ever could. The little animal's ears flitted to and fro, her haunches working as she dragged the tiny cart through the street at a brisk jog. Even where the streets grew dark for lack of street lamps as they approached the slums, the donkey's pace didn't slow.

"I'm always amazed at how surefooted she is," said Tilly, looking over at Micah. There was not quite enough space for the both of them on the front seat of the cart, but Tilly liked it that way. She liked how close to Micah she had to sit, how she could almost feel the heat of him against her.

His smile flashed, dazzling in the darkness. "Magi is an old hand. She knows these streets better than I do," he said. "She's nearly twenty years old, you know."

"Nearly twenty," said Tilly, impressed.

"That's the only way I could afford to buy her and the cart." Micah laughed, touching Magi's rump with the whip in a gentle manner, like a caress. "The poor old thing was going for a song at the sale when I was looking for a new handcart. I knew the knacker man had his eye on her, but she just seemed to have more left to give. And it's much easier than pushing the handcart."

Tilly smiled up at Micah, loving his compassion. It was several weeks since he'd found her again, and the more time she spent with him, the more she grew to realize how deeply she was attracted to his kindness.

"Well, I truly appreciate your effort in taking me home each night," she said gently.

"Oh, it's right on my way to my own flat," said Micah easily. "I couldn't bear to think of you walking all that way home every night."

"It was exhausting," Tilly admitted. She didn't tell him that it was also terrifying, when she feared so deeply that Bert might be around every corner. It was such a silly fear. She didn't want to mention it to Micah. He would think her mad, and then maybe things between them would be over as quickly as they had started.

"And besides." Micah smiled at her, his voice dropping an octave so that she felt it vibrate in her chest. "It's always good to spend time with you."

She smiled up at him, and for a moment, it seemed as though he might lean down and kiss her. But of course, not here, in the streets. And they were turning down the street to her tenement in any case. Tilly fought back a quick dash of disappointment, startled at how sharply and suddenly she had longed for him.

Micah stopped the donkey in front of the building, and Tilly stepped down. "Thank you, Micah," she said. "I'll see you tomorrow night."

"And then it's almost Sunday." Micah beamed. "Shall I bring sausages and chips for the children again?"

"Oh, they would love that," said Tilly. The children were falling in love with Micah too, and not just because he always brought them a square meal on a Sunday afternoon.

"Wonderful. Then I'll see to it." Micah winked. "Goodnight, Tilly."

"Goodnight," said Tilly softly.

She stood in front of the tenement for longer than was really necessary, watching Micah's cart disappear into the darkness.

Clasping a hand over her chest, she closed her eyes, relishing the delicious warmth she felt inside. It had been so long since anything had really awoken this feeling inside her: a feeling not only of love, but also of hope, of looking forward to something. She took a deep breath, savouring it for a second. Joy was hard to come by. She had to appreciate every bit of it that she could find.

Sighing with contentment, Tilly turned around to go into her tenement building and bumped straight into Bert Carter.

He smiled at her, a loose-lipped grin that never touched his unfocused grey eyes.

"Hello, Tilly," he said.

Tilly screamed. It was a sound that boiled up from a dark place she never visited, something harsh and primal, an instinctive cry of utter fear that was cut off short when Bert slapped his hand over her mouth and drove his body against hers, slamming her against the wall with a force that knocked stars over her vision.

"You're still a pretty little thing," he hissed in her ear, his breath hot and urgent. "I wish you'd have been cleaner, but after all this time, I know you'll do." One hand remained clamped sharply over her mouth; the other was seeking her hips, her thighs, creeping up her dress toward places no one had touched since Ray, trampling over the sacred boundaries, desecrating that which was most intimately her own.

Tilly tried to scream, but only managed a muffled sound against Bert's hand. He chuckled, the reek of alcohol on his breath. "Don't struggle," he whispered. "My little daughter died this fall. The flu took her. You're all I have left now. Don't deny me that."

He had found the edge of her skirt now, and he was struggling with it, trying to hitch it up over her knees with one hand while the rest of him leaned against her, crushing her against the wall with such force she could hardly breathe. Darkness swarmed the edges of her vision, nausea rising in her throat, and all she could think was that she hoped the children had not heard her scream and would not see her now −

"Let her go."

Micah's voice was almost unrecognizable, raised in a throaty roar of animal rage that tore through Tilly's fading conscious-ness. Suddenly the hand was gone from her mouth and skirts, and they fell blessedly back to her ankles where they belonged, and Tilly crumpled to her knees, gasping for breath, drooling and vomiting with shock and pain at what had so nearly happened. There were grunts and screams from around her, but it took her a few moments to clear her mind and vision and see what was happening right in front of her.

Micah was on the ground. Bert, straddling his chest, his lips loose in a grimace of anger, his fists flying again and again and again into Micah's face. Bert's fists were slick with blood; Micah was trying to resist, throwing up his hands, scrabbling uselessly at Bert's face and neck as blow after blow rained down into his face. Even as Tilly watched, Micah stopped resisting, his hands falling limply to his chest.

"No," Tilly shrieked. "NO!"

She didn't think. She just rushed at Bert, locked her hands around his neck and dragged him backwards off Micah with a strength she didn't know she had. He tumbled to the ground at her feet, and for a fleeting moment she wanted to kick him, to pound her feet into him with all her strength. But she hesitated, and he rolled to his feet and looked up at her with a fury in his eyes that struck cold terror deep into her soul.

"What's going on out here?" shouted a crotchety old voice, and Tilly's shoulders sagged with relief. She'd never been so relieved to hear Mrs. Gottun's voice in her life. Glancing back, she saw that every window and door was open on the building, everyone looking down at the commotion.

She looked back at Bert. His eyes bored into hers.

"You're mine," he growled. "This isn't over."

Then he turned and bolted, and Micah let out a small, breathy sound that lanced right through Tilly's heart. It sounded like a cry for help. She hurried to him, fell to her knees beside him, and her heart was breaking. Her dear, dear Micah was unrecognizable, his lips bleeding, his temples torn, his eyes already swollen almost shut.

"It's all right," Tilly gasped. She wrapped her arms around him, hoisted him into her arms. "It's all right, my love. I'm here. I'm here."

"Tilly," Micah groaned out. His eyelids fluttered; a limp hand found her cheek, smearing it with blood. "Are you..." His sentence ended in a moan of pain.

Tilly knew at that moment that she was in love with him. The moment when, through his own horrifying pain, he was concerned for her above all else.

"I'm fine," said Tilly. "I'm fine, my sweetheart."

"Did he..." Micah stopped. He seemed to be fighting to keep his eyes open.

"No," said Tilly. "You saved me. He didn't." Tears spilled down her cheeks.

Micah let out a sigh then, his head lolling back. And no matter how she screamed his name, or kissed his bloody cheeks, or hugged him to her, he didn't wake up. She clutched him then, her face buried in his neck, just feeling the steady thump of his heart against her chest, praying with all of her might that it would keep on beating.

CHAPTER 13

TILLY'S LIMBS trembled with exhaustion as she stumbled down the steps to her tenement. She had forgotten how exhausting it was to walk back from the Hambright mansion every day; it had been two weeks since Micah had convinced her she had no choice but to sell Magi and the cart on his behalf, and while she was glad of the money, she could hardly keep her eyes open now. It was after midnight. At least she had a small bag of coal and another of vegetables with her; the burden had been overwhelmingly heavy to carry, but she was grateful for it.

"I'm home," she called softly, walking into the room. Robby and Lissa lay on one pallet, their arms wrapped around each other, fast asleep. Janie was crouched beside the other pallet, where Micah's tall figure lay wrapped in a blanket. His eyes were closed, and Tilly felt a nasty pang of fear as she set down the coal and vegetables.

"He's asleep, Mama," Janie said softly, looking up at her. "I'm glad of it."

"Did he have a bad day?" Tilly asked quietly. She sat down beside Janie, wrapped an arm around her and kissed her forehead. How could one depend so heavily on one's own child? She didn't know what she would have done without Janie.

"He moaned a lot," said Janie. "And sometimes he was very confused."

The doctor at the free clinic, whom Tilly had visited when she still had the donkey and cart to use, had told her this was to be expected. He had said that Micah should really be in hospital. But who had money for that? Besides, Tilly doubted that strangers would care for him the way she did. Still, the doctor had said that with time and rest, Micah would recover. Looking at his thin, pale face, twisted with pain even in sleep, Tilly could only hope that this was true.

"Let's do some reading, love," she said, kissing Janie on the cheek. "Find our place in the newspaper and then we'll read while I get supper ready."

Janie went off obediently despite the late hour—for the children were used to it, and in the comparative privacy of the back corner of the room, Tilly leaned down and pressed her lips very gently to Micah's forehead, relishing his unique smell. She took his limp hand and squeezed it gently; there was warmth to it now, at least, and he let out a deep sigh as though he was sleeping peacefully.

"Just rest, darling," Tilly whispered. "Just rest."

She looked up to meet the baleful glare of Mrs. Gottun, who was standing in the gap in the wall, her arms crossed. Tilly gritted her teeth, fighting the urge to snap at her. She knew that Mrs. Gottun disapproved of Micah's presence, but at least it hadn't gotten Tilly evicted so far.

She pushed the fear of eviction down on her list of worries, concentrating instead on making a watery vegetable soup for supper while she kept half an eye on Micah and listened to Janie reading to the others. Even though Micah was asleep, there was something cosy about having him in the tenement. Despite her bone-deep tiredness, Tilly found it in her to enjoy it.

She fed the children first and put them to bed, then took a bowl of soup and crouched beside Micah's pallet. Laying a hand on his shoulder, she squeezed it gently. "Micah, my love," she said softly, "it's time for supper."

Micah blinked. His eyes were sluggish at first, struggling to find her face, and Tilly feared that this would be one of those nights when he could barely recognize her. Then light dawned in his eyes, and a smile tugged at his swollen lips.

"Tilly," he croaked.

"Hello." Tilly bent and kissed his forehead again, not caring if it was appropriate or not. "Can you sit up?"

She helped him to sit, propping him against the wall; the movement made him breathless and dizzy, and he had to close his eyes and clench his jaw for a few moments until it passed. He was able to take the bowl and feed himself now, at least, even though his hand shook uncontrollably on the spoon. Tilly wondered if he would ever be able to work again. At least the sale of the donkey and cart had secured a few more weeks' rent for his own flat.

"Thank you," he said shakily, handing back the bowl. It was still half full.

"You need a little more, Micah," said Tilly gently. "You need to get your strength up."

He gave her a pained smile, but the love in his eyes was the same as always. "Tired," he breathed.

So Tilly fed him, spoonful by spoonful, and felt herself falling more hopelessly in love with him with every bite. When the soup was finished, she gave him his medicine and helped him to lie back down again. He closed his eyes and she expected him to sleep, but instead his hand found hers, closing around it.

"I wouldn't be alive if it wasn't for you," he whispered.

Tilly brushed his curls out of his face; they were growing wildly long now. "And my children wouldn't be alive if it wasn't for *you*," she said softly.

His eyes fluttered open with an effort, finding hers. "Thank you," he whispered. Painfully, his arm shaking, he reached up and brushed her cheek with his fingertips.

"You saved me," said Tilly. "I can never thank you enough."

"You..." He paused, grimaced in pain, took a deep breath and tried again. "You are enough."

The words were simple, but no one had ever said them to Tilly before, and they made things right inside her somehow in a way that nothing else ever had.

"Tilly?" he croaked. His voice was weak now, and Tilly had to bend down to hear him. "Yes?" she whispered.

He swallowed, the words coming out with sudden strength.

"I love you," he murmured.

Tilly leaned down, lay on the floor beside his pallet, rested her head on his chest. He wrapped an arm around her, and she listened to his thudding heart until it slowed and his breathing grew deep and quiet.

"I love you, too," she whispered.

MICAH STOOD among the dust of his workshop, the afternoon light pouring in through the small windows highlighting him from behind like some kind of angel. Golden motes danced around him every time he moved, twirling around his long curls, outlining his figure in brilliance. Tilly could only stare at him from the doorway for a few moments, almost forgetting to be worried as he moved among his disused equipment, touching a mould here, an anvil there.

It was so good to see him moving. Christmas was just around the corner, and the doctor had feared he might not walk again until New Year's, if at all. Tilly wished they still had the donkey cart so she could take him back to the good old doctor and show him how Micah had exceeded all of their expectations.

He turned to her, his smile splitting the golden afternoon. "It's all perfect." he said, beaming at her as he walked over to her. "Thank you, Tilly. You went to such efforts to make sure the rent was paid each week."

"Oh, Micah, I'm so glad everything is all right in here." Tilly smiled up at him. "You must be so happy to get back to work."

"Oh, I'm delighted," said Micah. He pulled open a drawer and started rummaging around in it among hammers and tongs, eventually finding a small cardboard box. "I feared I might not be able to work again at all."

"Me too," Tilly admitted. "But you're back now." She smiled up at him. He was still a little pale, his frame far thinner than she remembered, but there was health and vigour in his movements again. "I'm so happy for you."

Micah reached out, taking her hands. "I'm so happy for *us*," he said warmly.

Tilly glanced over her shoulder at the children. The door to the living area of Micah's flat was open, and the children were playing on the thin carpet, giggling.

"What do you mean?" she asked, raising her face to his.

He knelt in a sweeping movement, and Tilly's heart leaped into her throat. Holding up the tiny box, he opened it to reveal a tiny, plain iron ring. There were no precious stones, but a tiny heart design engraved into it.

She couldn't comprehend what was happening. Her eyes flitted from the ring to Micah's face and back.

"Tilly Barton." Micah squeezed her hand softly. "You have been a pillar of strength in my life these past few weeks. I could never stop thinking about you since the day I met you, and I've been waiting for this moment for two years." His voice lowered a little. "Will you marry me?"

Tilly's breath hitched in her throat. She looked into Micah's eyes, and she wanted to scream out her yes, to tap-dance on the Tower of London and shout it out to the world. But it caught in her chest.

"I... I don't know if I can," she said.

She saw something shatter behind his eyes, then clutched his hands, her voice urgent, desperate to make him understand. "Micah, I want to," she said, moving her hands to his dear face, kissing his cheek. "Please, don't misunderstand me. More than anything in the world, I want to marry you."

He stared at her, tears gathering in his eyes. "Then... then what's wrong?" he said.

"I don't know if we can legally get married," said Tilly. "Things... fell apart so badly after Ray. I never saw his death certificate. I... I don't know if I'm legally a widow."

"Oh." Micah's shoulders slumped with relief. "Well, we can find out, Tilly." He rose, drawing her up with him. "We'll make sure everything is right – and then I'll ask you again." He smiled, his tears disappearing. "At least now I know your answer...?"

Joy flared in Tilly's chest. It was all coming true. Her Christmas miracle. She threw her arms around his neck and laughed. "Yes." she said. "Of course, it's yes."

He leaned down and kissed her, and it was every dream Tilly had ever had, coming true all in one moment. Then he grinned down at her. "I'll keep this safe," he said, showing her the cardboard box. "Until everything is ready."

"Until then," Tilly agreed, and kissed him again.

TILLY WAS HUMMING to herself as she scrubbed the grate in the scullery. She had picked the tune of "Deck the Halls", and it was easy to hum, the melody trickling effortlessly out of her chest. The kitchen was brightly decorated with wreaths and holly; it was just days before Christmas, and Tilly's heart was full of joy.

"You're cheerful today," said Mrs. Scott, lifting a few loaves of bread from the oven. "What's gotten into you?"

Tilly looked up at her, trying to guess how Mrs. Scott would react. On one hand, she knew that few maids were married, but on the other, she would have to tell the cook eventually. Mrs. Scott was always in a good mood over Christmas. This seemed as good a time as any.

"Well," she said slowly, "my beau proposed to me yesterday."

Mrs. Scott raised an eyebrow at her. "And?"

"Well, I want to marry him, but I can't yet," said Tilly. "I haven't seen my first husband's death certificate yet. We have to save up for some time to get a solicitor to make sure, but once the legal things are sorted out, we're going to get married."

"Oh," said Mrs. Scott. "I hope you'll still be working here, because you're my best scullery-maid."

"Oh, ma'am, I will, I will," said Tilly quickly, "if you'll have me."

"Didn't you hear me, girl?" said Mrs. Scott grumpily. "You're a good scullery-maid. You might even make a tolerable enough kitchen maid." With that, she stumped off as though she hadn't just reassured Tilly of her job security and also hinted at giving her a promotion.

Tilly sighed with relief and went back to humming as she scrubbed, a smile tugging at her lips. Micah hoped to have enough money for a solicitor by February. Perhaps they could be married in the summer, and by next Christmas, she would be a married woman with a home again, and maybe the children could even go to the little church school. All would be well again. Best of all, she would be married to Micah, the most wonderful man she'd ever known. Micah was showing her not only what she'd missed when she was alone, but also what she'd missed even when she was married to Ray.

She had finished "Deck the Halls" and started on "God Rest Ye Merry Gentlemen" when the kitchen door burst open and a wide-eyed parlour-maid came bursting in. Tilly had resented Suzy a little at first for having such a high-paying job even though she was just seventeen, but it was hard to hate the wide-eyed, scatter-brained young girl with her sweet nature and gentle eyes.

"Tilly," she gasped. "You won't believe what I just heard."

Tilly smiled up at her. Suzy always had the best gossip in town. "Oh? What's that?" she said, glad of a little conversation while she scrubbed.

"They've just found three survivors of a dreadful shipwreck," Suzy cried.

Tilly winced. Even after two years and coming to terms with Ray's death, the word *shipwreck* still stung. "That's nice," she murmured.

"Tilly, you don't understand." Suzy rushed over to her, laying a hand on her shoulder. "Wasn't your husband lost at sea?"

Tilly forced a patient smile. "Yes, Ray was killed in a shipwreck," she said gently. "But it was a long time ago."

"Two years ago?" said Suzy.

Tilly looked up at her. "Yes."

"Tilly, these survivors have been living on one of the Scottish Isles for two years," said Suzy. "A fisherman just found them. They're calling it a Christmas miracle."

"I'm glad they survived, Suzy, but Ray is dead," said Tilly, unease filling her stomach.

"But he might not be. Oh, Tilly, allow yourself to hope," said Suzy. She glanced around the kitchen. "There's a newspaper here somewhere saying what ship it was – I'll show you."

Tilly lowered her head, continuing with her scrubbing and hoping with all her heart that Suzy wouldn't find that paper. She didn't want to reopen that old wound, or to face the feelings now boiling in her heart. She didn't know what she would feel even if Ray was alive, but she knew he wasn't, and she knew Suzy meant well, but she felt angry that the girl was insisting on showing her.

"Here," said Suzy breathlessly, waving a paper in Tilly's face. "It's right there. Look."

Tilly looked down, her eyes flitting through the article. She didn't recognize the name of the ship, and she was just about to feel relief when her eye caught a familiar word: *Carter*.

Tilly froze. She couldn't have read that right. It was impossible. But she had.

Albert James Carter, owner of the wrecked ship...

Tilly could no longer breathe. The scrubbing brush dropped from her fingers, and she collapsed to the floor, sobbing with all of her heart.

"I know. I know," Suzy cheered. "Your husband's alive, Tilly. He's alive."

But Tilly wasn't sure her tears were tears of joy.

CHAPTER 14

THE SHIP CAME sailing in on Christmas morning, but all the bells of heaven did not ring, and there were no angels singing. There was just Tilly, alone and terrified, having left her children with Micah. She couldn't forget the pain in his eyes when she had told him where she was going, or the utter guilt and confusion in her heart when she realized that all she wanted was to come back home to him and no one else.

Now, she didn't know if she was hopeful or terrified or angry or ashamed. She just knew that it was very cold, and the freezing wind stung the tears on her cheeks. She knew she could hardly see the ship coming slowly down the Thames through the impenetrable fog; only its outline sailed toward her, like a ghost ship coming in through the grey.

She knew the crowd was surging forward, a hushed silence falling over them, that the docks were bright with decorations, that someone was humming a Christmas carol nearby. Then she heard the creak of the gangplank, and a roaring cheer that shook the crowd. She couldn't wait any longer then. She started to shove through the crowd, pushing past angry men and hopeful women, praying that it was one of the other teary-eyed widows who was about to get her man back, hating herself for hoping that, wondering what kind of a person she was not to want her husband to be alive –

She stumbled out of the crowd, and there he was. His hair was wilder than she'd ever seen it, pouring down his shoulders, his beard reaching to his chest. She had never seen him with a beard before, or so very browned, or his eyes dark eyes quite so sharp and wild. But when he turned to her, she knew him instantly.

And she ran into his arms.

What else could she have done?

THINGS HAPPENED SO QUICKLY THEN. The papers were all over it. They were taking photographs and woodcuts, talking to Ray, talking to Tilly, wanting pictures of the children. Tilly's name was in the paper. No one mentioned Micah, except the children. Lissa and Robby didn't remember Ray. Janie didn't like him as much as she liked Micah and said so. Ray grew angry and shouted. Tilly cried.

Bert Carter had no choice but to pay Ray everything he had been owed for the two years he'd spent on the Scottish island, not with the papers swarming all over him, and Tilly was forced to look him in the eyes as he shook Ray's hand and congratulated him between clenched teeth before handing over the fat roll of banknotes.

Mr. Jones was all too happy to give them back the cottage and walking into it was like walking into a memory or perhaps a bad dream. The children, at least, were happy about the garden.

Tilly tried to be happy about the garden, or the children, or Ray, or anything. But all she felt was hollow.

THEY HAD BEEN in the cottage again for a week, and Tilly was sitting at the kitchen table that New Year's Day, watching the children build a snowman in the sunshine. They were warmly bundled up in the clothes Ray had bought for them at the slop shop, and Tilly herself couldn't remember the last time she'd had tea with real milk and sugar. She took another sip of it, listening to the children's laughter. It washed over her soothingly, like warm bathwater. Closing her eyes, Tilly thought about the hot bath she'd have again tonight. That was one luxury she could enjoy, she thought.

A hand descended on her back, making her jump. Tea slopped onto her lap, and she looked up in shock for a moment until Ray's familiar eyes met hers. He jerked his hand away as though she'd burned him.

"Ray." Tilly put a hand to her heart. "You startled me."

"Well, I'm sorry that I'd like to touch my wife, after being away from her for two years on a forsaken island," Ray snapped.

"Ray – I'm sorry." Tilly felt a wave of exhaustion and reached a hand toward him. "I'm just... getting used to things again, that's all."

Ray mellowed a little, taking her hand, and she glimpsed in his eyes the man she had once loved, or thought she loved. Had she ever felt about him the way she felt about Micah? Thinking about Micah while she was sitting here with him felt like adultery, and she forced him out of her thoughts, smiling at Ray instead.

"Things will get better, Tilly," he said, sitting down opposite her. "They'll go back to the way they always were." He frowned. "I just wish I understood why Bert wouldn't take me back."

Bert was another thing Tilly hadn't told Ray about. She could only hope he'd stay away from her now, but it was a slim hope, and she knew it. She feared what Ray would do if he ever found out.

"I'm sure you'll find other work," she said, trying to give him an encouraging smile.

"Oh, I will. Another captain will take me on." Ray grinned at her. "Then you could finally leave that dreadful manor. Really, Tilly, I don't understand why you insist on staying on." Frustration crept into his voice. "You know I'll find work again."

Tilly didn't know that, and that was why she'd kept her job at Hambright Manor even though she knew she'd become a spectacle after all the publicity of Ray's return apparently from the dead.

"It's just until you have work, darling," she said, stroking Ray's hand. "Then I'll leave, I promise."

This appeased him somewhat. He nodded to her. "This might be hard, but things will get better," he said. He frowned. "I just wish the children remembered me."

"Janie does," said Tilly. She forced another smile, working hard to make things right between them. "And besides, it won't matter that they don't have any old memories if you work hard to make new ones."

Ray's face brightened. He followed her gaze outside, to where the children were playing. "You're a clever girl, Tilly," he said, "and you're quite right." He jumped to his feet. "I'm going to go and build that snowman with them."

Maybe she could fall back in love with him, after all. "That's a good idea."

"Thank you. You're a darling," he said, leaned down, and kissed her full on the mouth. Tilly did her best not to flinch.

She sat at the table for a little longer, sipping her tea and watching them. Robby was hanging back; Lissa was just happy that someone had agreed to give the snowman a scarf. Janie was making an effort to love him, Tilly noticed. She could only hope that the little girl would succeed, and maybe show her the way, too.

The knock at the door made her jump. Tilly sighed and got to her feet, brushing off her new dress. She could only hope it wasn't another writer for one of the papers.

It wasn't. It was Micah.

Tilly stood in the door for a long few seconds, staring up at him. Every cell in her body cried out for her to run into his arms, and it was only with the strongest of the resolve that poverty had built within her that she remained on that threshold, saying nothing.

He was the first to speak. Taking off his hat, he revealed his bouncing curls, sending agonizing pain through Tilly's heart.

"I didn't mean to intrude," he said, and swallowed. "Ma'am."

"Micah," said Tilly softly.

He held up a hand. "I'm not here for any trouble," he said softly. "I... I just wanted you to know, that's all." Micah struggled to smile. "I just had something to tell you."

Tilly bit her lip, dropping her eyes to her feet. "Micah, I'm so sorry," she whispered.

"No. Please. That's why I'm here." Micah reached for her, stopped, let his hand fall to his side. "I don't want you to be sorry. I want you to know that I'm truly, truly glad for you."

She raised her eyes to his. There was nothing but genuine compassion in his eyes, the kind of boundless love that made him everything she'd ever wanted.

"Getting Ray back is a miracle, Tilly," said Micah softly. "You deserve every Christmas miracle in the world. I wanted to tell you to enjoy it – to live it to the full." He gave her a faltering smile. "I want you to take in all this joy, as though the last two years never happened, and go back to your life the way it used to be. I want you to know I'll be just fine." His voice broke on the last syllable.

"Micah…" Tilly began, not knowing what to say.

"No." Micah stepped back, tears glittering in his eyes. "I mean it, Tilly. Live your life. Enjoy it." He swallowed hard. "Forget about me."

He turned and walked away, and Tilly watched him go, wishing she could. For one thing was certain.

She would never forget Micah Connoly.

PART III

CHAPTER 15

ONE YEAR Later

THE WALK from the Hambright mansion to the cottage took more than an hour, and it was after eleven at night by the time Tilly finally left the manor houses behind and joined the flood of factory workers heading toward home in the streets surrounding her own. She could barely keep her eyes open. Her feet ached, but they still seemed a long way away from her head, as though she was floating on a wave of tiredness.

This was nothing new. And she still had to make supper. The thought made Tilly's heart fail within her, so she pushed it aside, trying not to think about anything at all. Instead, she focused on the falling snow, brilliantly white in the light of the street lamps as it fell through the still air, yet turning ghastly grey and yellow once it reached the dirty pavement. The only place it stayed beautiful was where it landed on the wreaths and evergreens hanging from every building, dusting it all with a picturesque layer of white flakes, like icing sugar. There was a great Christmas tree in front of the bakery, gingerbread figures swinging gently from it in the soft breeze.

She tried to think about the decorations and the snow, but her thoughts kept dragging back to the same place they always did when she was exceptionally tired on one of the long walks home. She thought longingly of the donkey cart, and of sitting next to Micah, squashed against him on the tiny seat. Of the way his eyes sparkled. Of his smile...

Tilly shook her head so forcefully she stopped in her tracks. She was married to Ray, her miraculous Ray, back from the dead. That was good enough for her, so why did she dream of an ironsmith she could never have?

Her eyes scanned dully over the bustling street, as though vaguely hoping she might spot him standing somewhere on a street corner. Of course, she didn't. She hadn't seen him since New Year's Day, and that was almost a year ago now.

She turned to keep walking, and that was when she spotted it: the flash of movement beside the bakery, as of a burly figure darting into an alley. Tilly froze. She could swear she had seen the same thing yesterday – something like a man ducking out of sight, right in that spot. Surely, it couldn't be...

Tilly shook her head again. The ghosts of the past just wouldn't let her ago, especially not at this time of year, but it was time for her to focus on her present. She turned and plodded toward home.

❦

TILLY COULD HEAR the angry muttering even before she opened the cottage door. She paused on the threshold, exhausted beyond all measure, and stood there waiting for strength to fill her from some unknown quarter. Dully, she noticed that the wreath on the front door was starting to wilt a little with a few days still to go before Christmas. They'd cut it from the oak tree and decorated it with bits of holly that dear old Polly had given them, because there was no money for a proper wreath this year.

There was no money for anything except food and rent, and even that was only because Tilly was still working for the Hambrights. She had hoped that things would get better now that Ray had found a job cleaning fish on the docks. Instead, it only seemed to make him angrier, and she could hear him complaining loudly in the kitchen even through the closed door.

Tilly took one more moment to steel herself. Then she stepped through the door and into the kitchen, forcing brightness into her voice. "I'm home, my darling."

Ray looked up. He was sitting at the kitchen table, and when he looked up at her, his eyes still held the wildness that had come home with him from the Scottish Isles. She wished it would leave him, but she knew it wasn't the reason why things were different between them. Shredded paper lay all over the kitchen table, and Tilly blinked at it for a moment before Ray spoke.

"You took your time," he said. "Janie put supper on."

"Janie is a brick," said Tilly, noticing the bubbling pot on the coal stove. She went over to him and kissed him dutifully on the cheek. "How was your day, my darling?"

Ray shook his head. "I was cleaning fish, Tilly," he said shortly. "I would have liked the open sea better."

Maybe he had always liked the open sea better than her and the children, Tilly thought, but she was glad he wasn't on it now. She had been praying quietly that she would never have to see him set sail again, even if it meant cleaning fish would be his fate.

She went over to check on the pot. It was fish stew again – it was always fish stew lately; part of Ray's wages each week was a few portions of the fish that his master couldn't sell – but Tilly was just glad she hadn't had to make it herself.

Ray's tone suggested he had relented a little. "How about you?" he asked. "Were you all right today?"

"I was just fine." Tilly forced a smile.

"Did you ask them about having Christmas Day at home with your family?" Ray asked.

"I... I asked Mrs. Scott, but she said she would think about it." Tilly felt her chest tighten with pressure. "But they're having a dinner party, and..."

"Of course, they are." Ray shook his head. "Rich folk just can't see us as human beings at all." He snorted. "Just like that dreadful swine, Bert Carter, hiring the other two sailors but leaving me to starve even though I was nearly killed on that ship of his."

Tilly said nothing. Ray didn't know the half of it, and she wanted to keep it that way. She didn't want to think of what he'd do if he found out about Bert. It would land him in prison, and for Ray to end up in prison after all he'd been through... it didn't bear thinking about.

She gestured to the scraps of paper on the table. "What's this?"

"Nothing," Ray snapped.

Tilly put a hand on his shoulder, forcing down her frustration and filling her tone with love instead. "You can tell me, my love," she said softly. "I want to help."

Ray lowered his face into his hands, running his fingers through his thick, dark hair.

"Mr. Jones is raising the price of rent again," he muttered.

Tilly felt the ground wobble beneath her feet, but she took a deep breath to hide her shock. They had survived on Tilly's pitiful wage as a scullery-maid for months before Ray had found work. They could survive on both, even if the rent was raised.

"It'll be all right, love." Tilly wrapped her arms around him, cradling him, willing it to start to feel natural, like it had been in their newlywed days. The days before Micah. "It'll be all right," she repeated, loudly, as if to drown out her thoughts.

As if that would help her forget that Micah Connoly had ever existed.

TILLY WAS TOO tired to haggle with the grocer, but she was well aware his price for a single cabbage was ludicrous. Ray had given her a strict budget for her Sunday afternoon grocery trip. It was the way things had always been, of course; in years past, Ray had always been the one bringing home the money, and he had set the budget, which Tilly had been only too pleased to gratefully follow. But now that most of their money was coming from her work, Tilly was starting to struggle with resentment over being told how to spend her own wages.

She forced away the feeling, managing a thin-lipped smile for the grocer. "Is that the price of two cabbages, sir?" she said trimly, giving him an opportunity to negotiate.

Instead, he laughed. "Oh, no, ma'am, that's the price of one. But for a pretty lady like you, I might throw in another at a lower price."

It seemed such a harmless compliment, but Tilly snapped her purse shut, a desperate chill running through her body. She didn't want strangers to tell her she was pretty or offer her things because they found her attractive. Her beauty was meant for only one man, and that was her husband. If only other men could see it that way.

"Good day to you, sir," she said icily, turning away from his stall.

The grocer called out after her, but she ignored him, moving on instead to a stall selling cheeses. It was all hung with red and green bunting, with bright red ribbons tied to the corners of the stall and strings of holly and mistletoe scattered on the table among the cheeses. Tilly loved cheese, and these were huge and golden, but Ray hadn't given her a budget for cheese. She paused by the stall nonetheless, gazing at the great wheels, some of them waxed in all different colours. Why was she lingering? It was her only afternoon of rest, and she could be putting her feet up at home.

But it was a nice enough day, she supposed, the sky very low and grey, yet no wind blew. And Tilly didn't want to go home. It was so much too complicated there. Besides, she could see her children playing with a group of others in the middle of the market square, and they seemed to be enjoying themselves so much. They were playing in the shadow of a tall Christmas tree all decked out in ribbons and white candy canes and gingerbread men; in a few days, a jolly old man in a red suit, this year's Father Christmas, would be visiting to give hand-picked brown paper parcels to the children whose parents could afford this. Tilly would have to be careful to keep her own children away.

She lingered by the stall, watching them, feeling joy warming her heart. They were the one thing that made her truly happy at this time. It was so good to see Janie with round, red cheeks, and Lissa laughing, and Robby smiling and playing and participating for once. He was busy forming a snowball in his hands, the snow crusting on his knitted mittens, his eyes dancing. Tilly remembered when Ray's eyes had been soft and bright like this, too. Had she ever really been in love with him?

She was thinking of their wedding day, and of how excited she had been, when she heard a warm voice talking behind her. "Pam, it's so good to see you. How are the children?"

She closed her eyes, her back to the cheese stall, and listened to that voice. It was warm and deep, just like Micah's had been. It wouldn't be him, of course – he had been avoiding her for the past year – but it was good to listen to it anyway, even though it felt wrong.

"They're well, thank you, young sir," said the stallholder's old country voice. "I must thank you again for buying that new wheel for my cart. Why, I would never have been able to get out of London without it."

"Not at all. I'm glad I did, considering it was while I was replacing the wheel that you told me you were moving to a different marketplace." There was a chuckle, and that, too, was eerily familiar; so familiar that goosebumps rose on Tilly's skin. "Now, tell me, do you have some of that cheddar I love?"

"Always for you, Mr. Connoly," said the stallholder.

Connoly. Tilly felt her breath hitch in her throat. She knew she should walk away, get the children and go home to her husband, but even as she knew this, she was already turning around.

"Micah?" she whispered.

It was him, looking tall and strong again, with healthy colour in his cheeks, the scar on his forehead so faded that she wouldn't have known it was there if she hadn't been looking for it. And his eyes were the same, of course, always the same, filled with such warmth and light that they took Tilly's breath away.

"Tilly?" he said, looking as dumbstruck as she felt.

All of her cried out to run into his arms, but she didn't. She just clutched her purse in front of her, fiddling with the clasp. "You look so well," she said.

"I *am* well, thanks to you." Micah smiled at her, and it was almost impossible to resist that smile. "Are the children here?"

"Yes – playing over there," said Tilly. "I can call them..."

"No." Micah held up a hand. "Better not." There was sorrow in his eyes, but Tilly felt a wave of enormous respect for this man, knowing how desperately he wanted to see those children and also knowing, as she did, that seeing him again would only cause more questions just as they were starting to settle into their new lives with their old father figure. "It's still nice to see you, though," Micah offered.

His voice was oddly flat. Tilly wondered if there was a new Mrs. Connoly yet, then thrust the thought angrily from her mind. That was none of her business.

"It's nice to see you, too," she said. "Have you been... happy?" She felt a sudden urge to know this; as if knowing that Micah was happy was enough to make up for her lack of that joy.

He gave her an unreadable, flickering smile. "Yes," he said.

Tilly was relieved, yet something hurt inside her at the same time. She wished she could do what Micah had done – find a new way to be happy. Part of her wanted to tell him everything, to tell him she was still in love with him, that the way her heart pounded now as she looked at him was irrefutable proof of this. But she couldn't. She was married.

"I should go," he said, paying Pam for the cheese. "It really was lovely to see you, Tilly."

"You too," Tilly breathed.

She watched him go until the crowd swallowed him, and the hollow ache in her chest that she had been feeling ever since she had had to leave him continued, strong enough to take her breath away.

THE CHILDREN CLAMOURED AROUND TILLY, chattering excitedly about Christmas as she walked home at last late that afternoon with two heavy parcels in her arms – the week's groceries, plus the small bag of bread that Janie was carrying. Janie was the only one who didn't seem to be viewing this coming Christmas with any kind of excitement. She was quiet as she followed close beside Tilly, while Lissa and Robby bounced all over the street.

"I can't wait for my dollhouse," Lissa cried. "Papa said it would be this big." She stretched out her arms, her eyes dancing. Tilly wondered if she had fallen so thoroughly in love with Ray because or in spite of the fact that she didn't remember him from before the shipwreck.

"And I can't wait for my bicycle," said Robby, jumping into the air. "I'll be so fast. I could go anywhere. Why, Mama, you could use it to go to work, too, if you wanted." He quieted a little, taking Tilly's hand.

She couldn't help but smile at his sweetness, though she wished Ray would stop promising the children that Father Christmas would bring them such things. It would only lead to disappointment on Christmas morning. "That's nice of you, dear," she said.

They had left the marketplace behind and were passing the little church where all three children had been baptized and Ray and Tilly had gotten married. It was bright with decorations now, Advent candles shining in the windows, the bright sound of Christmas carols coming from within. *O come all ye faithful, joyful and triumphant.* Tilly wished she could find joy and triumph in Christmas again.

She was gazing at the church, her heart filled with nostalgia, when she saw it again. A flitting of movement. Someone ducking around the corner of the church, disappearing into the courtyard behind it. She paused.

"Mama, what's wrong?" asked Janie instantly.

Tilly moved a little closer to her daughter. "Nothing, Janie," she said quietly. "Nothing at all."

She stared to move on, but just as she reached the bottom of the street, she could not contain her fear and had to look back toward the church one more time. This time, he wasn't quick enough. She saw him standing in the corner of the church grounds, looking at her over the hedge, a disembodied head floating above the bright holly and the snow, and even from this distance she knew him at once. She would never forget that face. She would never forget the terrible grimace upon it as he drove his fists into Micah's face.

A parcel dropped from Tilly's hands, landing on the street with a thump, turnips and carrots rolling every which way. Janie and Robby dived to save them, and Tilly looked away for just one moment, mumbling something about her clumsiness, desperate for her children not to notice the way her hands were shaking uncontrollably.

When she looked back, it was already too late. Bert Carter was gone.

CHAPTER 16

TILLY SOMEHOW MANAGED to keep it together on the rest of the walk home. She couldn't tell the children what she had seen, she knew they would know only inconsolable terror if she told them that Bert Carter was following her just as she had feared. They didn't know the whole story, of course. No one but Micah knew that.

And now Ray would have to know. The thought made Tilly's stomach clench, but she had to tell him. She had to keep her children safe. And what might Bert do to Ray, if he followed Tilly home?

For the thousandth time, as they approached her cottage, Tilly looked over her shoulder. The street was cold and silent and empty, wreaths on all the doorways, snowmen in the gardens, Christmas trees shining through living room windows. What had once seemed cosy was now merely cold. There were so many places he could hide.

"Mama, what's wrong?" said Janie pleadingly.

Tilly didn't even try to force a smile. She knew there was no hiding anything from Janie.

"Go inside, darling," she said. "Everything is going to be all right."

It was a relief when the children had all tumbled into the kitchen, and Tilly could close the door firmly behind them. She let out just half a breath, looking through the window into the garden. It was empty. The children would be safe enough there. "Why don't you all go and play in the garden, children?" she said, her voice shaking audibly.

"But Mama, we're hungry," said Lissa.

"Just for a little while, silly." Janie grabbed Lissa's hand. "While Mama gets supper ready, right, Mama?"

Janie met Tilly's eyes, and for the millionth time, Tilly wondered how she would ever have survived without Janie. "That's right," she said. "Off you go."

Janie led the younger ones out into the garden, glancing over her shoulder one more time as she stepped through the front door, and Tilly hurried at once to her bedroom. It was a glorious relief to open the door and see Ray sitting at the little writing desk against the window, painstakingly buffing his shoes.

"Ray, my love?" she said, closing the bedroom door.

He looked up at her, a brief smile crossing his features. "You're home. That took a long time. Is everything all right?"

"It was busy at the market square," Tilly lied. She swallowed hard. "But no... my love, everything is... is not... all right." The tears overwhelmed her, and she covered her face with her hands and sobbed, weeping in absolute fear, her body trembling uncontrollably, her belly burning with terror.

"Tilly." Ray hurried over to her, alarmed. She thought he might pry her hands away from her face at first, but instead he threw his arms around her and drew her close to his chest. He didn't hold her like this often. She felt sincerity in his embrace now, and returned it, clinging to him, burying her face in his shoulder. It felt good. It felt so good to lean against him and hold him, and for that one instant, she finally did it. She forgot all about Micah.

"Tilly, my sweet, what on earth is the matter?" Ray stroked her hair, still holding her tightly. "You look as though you've seen a ghost."

"I... I almost have." Tilly lifted her face, staring pleadingly into his eyes. "Oh, Ray, I didn't want to tell you... but... but we're in danger. We're in awful, awful danger." She thought of the brutality with which Bert had pounded Micah's face, and the thought of the same thing happening to Ray brought on a fresh wave of helpless, terrified tears.

"Danger?" Ray held her shoulders in his hands, pushing her gently back to look into her eyes. "You're not making any sense, my love. Who would want to harm us?"

"Bert," Tilly choked out. "Bert Carter."

Ray stepped back. "What?"

Danger glinted in Ray's eyes, and Tilly felt a pang of horror. She just wanted to keep Ray safe. Had she done the wrong thing? She clutched his hands, looking desperately into his eyes, and began to plead with him.

"Darling, please, please, whatever you do, you must promise me that you won't do anything foolish when I tell you what happened last Christmas," she said. "Please, Ray, you can't. Please. Promise me. Promise me or I can't tell you. You must stay calm, my love, please, you must, you must." She dissolved into tears of helpless fear.

"All right, all right. Come on, Tilly, you've got to tell me," said Ray.

"Promise me," Tilly sobbed. "Promise me."

Ray shook his head, as if in shock. "All right. I promise. Now tell me."

Tilly's eyes flooded with tears. She felt she could no longer stand; her knees wobbled, and Ray guided her gently to their bed, where she sat on the edge and wept, the words coming out in fragments between sobs. She told him about Bert's visit to their home when Ray had first gone missing, and about the "favours" he had asked for when she'd gone to his offices hoping for payment.

"That dirty scoundrel," Ray snarled.

"You promised," Tilly begged him. "Please."

"Keep talking," Ray growled.

She told him then about coming home to find Bert in the kitchen, and Ray began to tremble with anger, his eyes dark and blazing. But it was only when she told him about the day Bert had found her in front of her tenement, and how close he had come to having his way with her, that Ray shot to his feet.

"I'll kill him," he cried, his voice hoarse with rage. "I'll kill him."

"Ray, please." Tilly gasped, grabbing his arm. "You promised you would be calm. You promised. You *promised.*"

"I'll kill him," Ray shouted. He ripped his arm from Tilly's grasp and stormed out of the bedroom, slamming a hand against the door so hard that it smacked back on its hinges.

"Ray, no!" Tilly shrieked. She rushed after him; he was already out of the front door, storming down the street. She was about to run after him when she heard a cry from behind her.

"Mama. What's happening?"

She turned to see Janie standing in the kitchen door, tears glittering on her cheeks, naked fear in her eyes. She was only nine years old, Tilly realized with a shock, and right now she looked it.

"Stay here," Tilly shouted at her.

"But Mama – "

"Janie, stay here," Tilly barked. "And lock the door."

She slammed the front door shut behind her and started running up the street, just in time to see Ray holding up a hand on the street corner, flagging down a cab he couldn't afford. She shouted his name until her throat felt as though it would bleed, but he had already gotten into the cab and yelled something to the driver, and the horse scrambled recklessly into the falling twilight, breaking into a gallop as it disappeared down the street.

"NO," Tilly screamed. "Ray. RAY!"

She waved her arms wildly, desperate for a cab to stop, neither knowing nor caring how she would pay him, simply desperate to get to Ray, to stop him.

Before he did something terrible.

THE CAB RIDE to Bert's offices was the longest few minutes of Tilly's entire life. Time seemed to slip by like syrup, even though the cabbie – a round-faced, kind-eyed man who had blessedly taken mercy upon Tilly at the sight of her desperate tears – was driving the horse as quickly as he could. The animal's hooves struck sparks on the stones, its flanks lathered with sweat, the cab hurtling this way and that in the slow Sunday traffic as Tilly was thrown around in the back of the cab. She clung to her seat, leaning out of the window, desperate for a glimpse of Ray's cab up ahead. But it had taken her several minutes to find a cab, and try though the cabbie might, his horse's face was grey with age. They just couldn't keep up.

After an interminable age of darting through traffic and crashing wildly through bumps and holes, Tilly finally smelled the Thames, and they were approaching Bert's offices. She could hear a rising commotion, like the roar of waves up ahead, and a cold hand clutched at her heart.

She couldn't be too late. Surely, someone would have stopped him.

"Here, cabbie," she cried out when the flashy glass doors with their big bronze letters came into view.

The cab skidded to a frantic halt in front of the office. If Tilly had hoped that Bert wouldn't be at the office so late on a Sunday afternoon, her hopes were dashed: there were carriages everywhere, flashy ones with plumes on the horses' harnesses, men in top hats and tailcoats, ladies in bright gowns. There must have been some kind of office gathering. Tilly's heart was in her mouth.

She threw herself from the cab. "Godspeed, ma'am," shouted the cabbie.

But she wasn't fast enough. She knew it as soon as she heard the screams, as soon as she saw the wide-eyed shock on the faces of the men and women gathered on the pavement outside the offices, as soon as she heard the shrill whistles of policemen and the clatter of hooves coming nearer. She knew it as soon as she saw the size of the crowd that was gathering outside the offices. When she saw the man with the blood-stained handkerchief held to his head, heard his panicky voice: "I tried to stop him. I tried."

There was broken glass on the ground. Tilly shoved through the crowd, her feet crunching upon it, until she reached the ruined facade of the building. It looked as though a bull had charged through the front door; it had swung back on its hinges, and there was shattered glass everywhere, speckled with the remnants of the bronze lettering.

There was a man by the door, and when Tilly rushed toward it, he tried to catch at her sleeve. "Madam, stop," he shouted. "There's – "

"He's my husband," Tilly shouted. She ripped away from him, screaming like an animal. "My *husband*."

She burst into the lobby; there was blood here, smeared on the floor, on the walls, and shrieking ladies collapsing to the ground, and wide-eyed men with pale faces, looking frozen with shock. And the sound. A meaty, pummelling sound.

But no screams. None at all.

She spotted Bert's burly form in the hallway, and it was as though no time at all had passed since his attack on Micah, because once again he was straddling a prone figure, once again he was slamming both fists down again and again, and there was blood on them, there was blood on the floor, there was blood everywhere. Tilly was slipping in it as she lunged at him, screaming and screaming and screaming, a wordless note of horror. The policemen were bursting through the door right behind her, but she reached Bert first just as he drew back his wrist for another blow. She grabbed his wrist, wrenching it back with all of her strength. But as soon as she looked over his shoulder and caught a glimpse of Ray, of her husband who had come back from the dead, she knew she was already too late. There was too much blood. His face was too contorted. Too crushed. Too... smashed in.

Bert struck at her. The blow landed across her face with an impact that turned the world black and filled her ears with a ringing sound. When the darkness lifted, a policeman was holding her in his arms, his eyes very wide as he stared down at her, and loud voices were shouting.

Tilly's mouth was full of blood. She had to spit some of it before speaking, reaching up with a trembling hand to grip at the young policeman's black uniform.

"Ray," she croaked out. "Ray. My husband."

The policeman looked up. Through her dizzy vision, Tilly saw two strong policemen holding down Bert. He was screaming, his cheeks flecked with foam, his eyes utterly wild. There was no humanity left in them anymore. There was nothing but hate.

"Ray," she croaked again.

Then she saw him. A doctor, with a little black bag, running through the crowd, toward the ruins of what had once been her husband. He fell to his knees beside Ray's body, touching his neck, his chest, what remained of his face.

Tilly shoved the policeman aside, staggering to her feet on wobbling knees. "Is he all right?" she gasped, tottering a step forward; her legs failed her, and she fell to her hands and knees, palms grating on broken glass. "Is Ray all right?" Her voice reached a hysterical pitch.

The doctor looked up. His lips sagged beneath his moustache. He shook his head.

Ray was not all right.

CHAPTER 17

TILLY HAD NEVER THOUGHT she would mourn the same husband twice.

This time, though, there was something to bury. There was absolute certainty, as she stood looking at the fresh grave, that Ray was in that coffin; the pounded pulp that was left of Ray after the brutal beating he had received from Bert Carter. The doctor had told Tilly, afterward, when her screaming and crying had given way to a silent shock in the wake of a medicine he had given her to calm her down, that Ray had been dead before she got there. Bert had pounded his brain to nothing in his terrifying fury.

Tilly had fought to stay strong through the funeral. But that had been yesterday, in front of the children. Now, she was alone; the children were still asleep, spent after yesterday, and she had walked the little distance to that self-same church where she and Ray had been married and where he now lay buried in the frozen ground. She knew he was dead, yet her mind kept thinking how cold he must be in that frigid earth, blanketed by snow. A thin powdering of it already lay on the fresh earth of his grave. Behind her, the church rocked with a joyous Christmas carol. The Christmas service was in full swing, and the congregation was belting out, "Good King Wenceslas". It was beautiful and joyous, so different from the ugly, agonizing turmoil in Tilly's heart.

She crouched down, laying a hand on the snow, digging her fingers into the loose dirt. The cascade of tears dripped down her cheeks, hot against the freezing wind.

"Oh, Ray," she whispered.

She wondered if it was her fault he was dead. No, not wondered: she knew. If only she had never told him about Bert, if only she had never gone to those offices, then Ray would still be alive. It was strange how she missed him now so passionately when she had been avoiding him only a few days ago. It was strange how she loved him better in death than she ever had in life.

Bitter tears coursed down Tilly's cheeks. How could she have lost him once, only to have him so cruelly snatched from her again? He had died right in front of her eyes. How could she recover from this? How could her children survive? They had lost Ray once, then Micah, now Ray again. Could they recover from so much loss in such a short time? Could she?

She wasn't even sure if she still had work. She'd have to move the children out of the cottage, back into that dreadful tenement beside Mrs. Gottun, if it even still existed. Tilly had had no contact with Mrs. Scott or the Hambrights; she could only hope they had read about her in the news. But even if she did still have work, how could she walk the streets of this hateful city after all that it had done to her?

"I thought I'd find you here, darling." A gentle hand descended on her shoulder.

Tilly squeezed her eyes tightly shut. Just as Polly had been there for her when Ray had first been lost at sea, so the old lady was right beside her now. It was a stroke of sheer luck that Polly was home at all; for the first time in years, she'd had to cancel her Christmas visit to her sister. Something about her sister's health. Tilly couldn't remember, but she was glad Polly was here, holding everything together.

"He's really gone this time, Polly," Tilly whispered.

"I know, my darling. I know." Polly squeezed her shoulder.

"Are the children all right?"

"They're fine," said Polly. "Playing in the garden. Lissa is talking about Christmas... I don't think she quite understands yet."

"And Janie?" said Tilly.

"She's trying to cheer up the youngsters. Robby's gone very quiet."

"I thought he would." Tilly wiped at her tears. "Oh, Polly, my poor, poor children." Bitter sobs clutched at her chest once more.

"Now, now, pet." Polly crouched down beside her, although Tilly knew it was difficult for the old lady to do so. "Calm yourself. I've brought some news – good news, I hope."

Tilly couldn't imagine any news that could be good now, but she looked at Polly attentively.

"They've hurried Bert Carter's trial right along," said Polly gently. "It wasn't difficult, not with all those eyewitnesses. The policeman stopped by your house just now and spoke with me. He says that they've convicted him. Carter will be punished for his many crimes, and he will never hurt anyone ever again. You never have to fear him again, Tilly."

Tilly wept; she wasn't sure if the tears were relief or despair, because it was all too late. The damage had been done. Bert had already killed Ray. How could she ever walk without fear again? How was there any way to come back from something like this? Polly pulled her to her feet and held her tightly as she cried, and Tilly clung to the old woman, feeling adrift on a sea of utter grief.

"Now, my sweet, I'm going to say something." Polly took hold of Tilly's shoulders, looking her in the eyes. "I want you to listen to me."

"Y-yes?" Tilly stammered.

"You need to get out of this city," said Polly. "You need to get away from all... all of this."

The thought had never occurred to Tilly. London was part of her very blood, yet as soon as Polly said it, she realized how desperate she was to escape it. The thought was unbelievably appealing.

"But where would we go?" Tilly whispered.

"You remember that I told you my old sister, Aggie, isn't well?" said Polly. "She's finding it very hard to walk, truth be told, and her useless son has been here in London for decades and doesn't have any interest in her. That's why I didn't go over there this Christmas – I didn't want to burden poor Aggie with another mouth to feed. But they need help, my pet, and you would be the perfect person to work for them. There's only a little bedsit, and not very much money; it would never have worked with Ray going along too. But Aggie loves children. They would brighten up the place, and I'm sure that if you agreed to work for your keep and the children's, they would hire you."

It all sounded like a dream; a distant future too good to belong to someone like her. Tilly stared at Polly. "Could... could that happen?" she breathed.

"It *will* happen, my dear," said Polly. "In fact, I've already written to Aggie. We'll all go over there after New Year's, if she agrees. I know she will."

Tilly wiped at her tears. A fresh start in the country, somewhere far away from Bert Carter and from the cottage and from all her painful memories. It sounded wonderful; perhaps this would be Christmas miracle enough for her.

"That would be wonderful, Polly," she said. "Oh... I don't know what I would do without you."

"Don't mention it, dear." Polly gave her a stiff little hug. "Now come on – let's go inside. You'll catch your death out here."

Tilly meekly followed the old lady away from Ray's grave and toward what might be a better future. She couldn't wait to leave London behind.

Even though, in the back of her mind, there was still the thought of Micah Connoly. Still the gentle longing for what might have been. But Micah had moved on. He was happy now. He'd told her so, hadn't he? And besides, he hadn't come to her when Ray was killed, and she was certain he had to have known. Hadn't it been in all the newspapers?

She drew in a long breath. It was time for her to find a way to be happy, too.

PART IV

CHAPTER 18

THREE YEARS Later

"SILENT NIGHT," Tilly sang quietly to herself, twisting the holly boughs a little tighter to make a circle. "Holy night. All is calm, all is bright." She tied off the ends of the holly and held the half-made wreath up to the pale winter's light filtering in through the large kitchen window. It was a truly massive kitchen; generations old, with giant flagstones and checkered curtains, and an oak table that seemed to have stood here for centuries. Perhaps the curtains were a little faded and the table in need of sanding, but there was still a stubborn old splendour about this farmhouse, something that Tilly had fallen in love with the moment she'd walked into the kitchen for the first time three years ago.

"That looks pretty, Mama," said Janie, who was kneading a lump of dough on the table beside Tilly.

"Thank you," said Tilly. "We'll brighten this old house right up for Christmas."

"Aggie will love that." Janie grinned. "Polly would have loved it, too."

Tilly returned her smile, feeling a faint tinge of grief, yet also warmth at the sweet memory of her dear old friend. Polly had enjoyed only one happy Christmas on the farm before she'd quietly slipped away in her sleep. Her last days had been utterly happy, and Tilly missed her, but she knew she was in a better place.

It was easier to miss Polly than it was to miss the only other person in her past that Tilly longed for. She pushed him out of her mind, reaching for a length of red ribbon to tie around the wreath.

"I'm sorry, Mama," said Janie. "I shouldn't have mentioned Polly."

"No, my love." Tilly reached over, wrapping an arm around Janie's shoulders, and hugging her close. Somehow, her little girl was the same height as Tilly. "Don't ever stop talking about Polly, or your papa, or anyone that you love and miss. It's good to remember them."

Janie smiled at her. "Lissa asked if we could make gingerbread tomorrow, after school."

School. Another glorious blessing that Aggie and her husband, Paul, had bestowed upon Tilly. They had sent the children to a little church school in the village and paid their meagre tuition. Janie was reading thick books from the library now instead of old scraps of newspaper.

"Of course," said Tilly warmly, "as long as you get to all of your chores first."

The kitchen door opened, and Tilly looked up to see a doddering old man enter, his head white, his back stooped. Aggie, who was Polly's double in almost every way, was holding on tightly to old Paul's arm. Tilly hurried to pull out chairs for them, Janie brought a blanket from where it hung beside the stove, and they made quick work of bundling up the old couple after their afternoon walk.

"There," said Robby, closing the door. He was ten now, and Tilly still was still struck every day by how much he looked like his father. "I didn't take them as far as normal, Mama, because it was getting cold."

"A good thing you brought us back when you did, young man." Aggie gave him a warm, gap-toothed smile. "My nose was about to drop off from the cold."

"It's almost midwinter," said Paul morosely.

"Oh, don't be such an old grump, darling." Aggie laughed, patting him on the knee. "It's almost Christmas, after all."

Paul brightened somewhat. "We'll have fattened goose," he said. "And plum pudding."

"Of course." Tilly smiled. "I've been waiting a long time with that plum pudding. Not to mention the fruitcake."

"And gingerbread," Robby chipped in.

Paul's eyes sparkled with delight. He loved Robby. "We won't forget the gingerbread, son," he said. "Hark at that wind. I think you'd best feed the pigs before it starts to snow."

"Yes, sir," said Robby, heading into the scullery adjoining the kitchen.

Tilly and Janie, with Lissa joining them from the scullery, quickly made cups of hot tea for the old couple and set out fresh biscuits for them. Everyone was talking happily, the kitchen filled with joyful voices. Tilly allowed the gentle joy to wash through her, embracing every second of it. She couldn't take any of this simple happiness for granted.

Aggie and Paul were creatures of habit, and their steady routine was always soothing. Once they'd finished their tea and biscuits, Lissa took them upstairs, where she had gotten the parlour ready for them to settle in and listen to her play the piano for half an hour or so. Aggie had been teaching her, and it wasn't long before the farmhouse was filled with soft music. Lissa had a natural ability with the piano, and though there were still faltering moments and the odd loss of key, the house soon echoed with the trickling notes of "O Christmas Tree".

Your boughs so green in summertime

Stay bravely green in wintertime

O tannenbaum, O Christmas Tree

How lovely are thy branches.

Tilly found herself humming along as she washed the cups and plates while Janie was busy chopping vegetables for supper.

"This was his favorite carol, you know," said Janie softly.

Tilly looked up. Janie's eyes were strangely vulnerable; great pools of liquid light in her pretty, pinched face.

"Oh, no, my dear," said Tilly, smiling. "I think your papa was partial to 'God Rest Ye Merry Gentlemen'."

"Not Papa." Janie bit her lip. "Micah."

The sound of Micah's name launched a sweet knife through Tilly's heart. She dropped her eyes to her work, fighting back the surge of emotion that had been coming to her more and more strongly every time Micah was mentioned. It startled her to know just how much she longed for him, after all these years.

"I suppose so," she said. "I don't really remember." But she did remember, of course. How could she forget even one single happy moment she had ever spent with him? She could hear his deep voice singing that carol now, warm and fine and booming.

"Why don't you talk about him, Mama?" said Janie. "You talk so often about Papa. Don't you miss him?"

Tilly sighed. "Yes," she said. "Every single day." She raised a hand to her heart, as though that could soothe the aching hole inside it.

"Then why don't you write to him?" said Janie. "We all miss Micah, you know, Mama. All of us loved him."

"Oh, darling." Tilly laughed. "You are silly. Micah's moved on. It's been four years, after all, since we were..." What? Courting? Almost engaged? Tilly broke off. "I pray every day that he's happy," she said, "and safe, and that he's enjoying Christmas with a pretty little wife."

"I don't think he could ever love anyone else the way he loved you," said Janie.

The thought was glorious, but Tilly couldn't allow herself to think it. Micah was in London, and London was cursed for her. She had only started finding happiness again when Polly had brought them here three years ago, and one thing was certain: Tilly would never go back. Especially not when she knew that Micah had long since forgotten her.

"You *are* fanciful, darling," said Tilly. "Get on with your work, now, and no more silly talk."

Janie gave her a steady look, then went back to cutting the vegetables. Tilly shook her head a little, as though to dislodge the deep yearning and quiet sorrow that had taken hold of her.

She was happy now. Alone, but happy. And that was better than anything she'd ever had back in London.

SQUEALS of joy echoed across the field beside the house and barn. Carrying a pail of fresh, steaming milk in each hand, Tilly walked across the yard, smiling at the sight of the children. They were having a spirited snowball fight in the field with some of the neighbours' children, laughing and shouting, snowballs flying. Even Janie, usually the picture of decorum, was launching a huge snowball through the air; it hit Robby squarely on the nose, engulfing his face with snow. The laughter doubled.

Tilly found herself laughing along with them, shaking her head as she turned to go back into the farmhouse. Her wreath was hanging on the door; she'd added a few old harness bells to it, so that there was a cheery jingle when she pushed the door open.

"Paul. Aggie!" she called. "You won't believe how much milk old Posy gave today. Why, I think there will be enough to make some cottage cheese tomorrow, and it'll be ready just in time for..."

Tilly stepped into the kitchen and was instantly startled by the presence of a tall man in a suit. She hadn't seen such a suit since leaving London, and between that and the leather brief-case in his hands, the man reminded her sharply of a London businessman. Her stomach turned, and she stared at him for a few moments, her eyes very wide.

"… Christmas." Tilly mumbled the end of the sentence, then looked over at Paul and Aggie. They were sitting at the kitchen table, and Aggie was crying, her head buried in wrinkled hands. Paul's arms were around her, and his face was utterly haggard.

"Wh-who are you, sir?" Tilly stammered, looking back up at the man in the suit with deep fright.

"I was just leaving." The man touched his hat to her. "Once again, Mr. and Mrs. Dowe, I apologize for the bad news."

He left, and Tilly hurried to the kitchen table, putting the two pails on the floor. "Paul? Aggie," she cried. "What is the matter? How can I help you? Are you ill?"

"No, no." Paul shook his grizzled old head, but his voice was breaking. "We're all right. Please make us some tea, Tilly. Poor Aggie has had a horrid shock."

"We both have," said Aggie. "Oh, Paul – oh, my poor, poor Michael. My poor Michael."

Michael was the name of their son, with whom they hadn't spoken in years. Tilly didn't know anything about him other than he was a businessman in London and had abandoned them in their old age.

She made the tea and set it out in front of them, and after a few hearty gulps of the tea, Aggie's tears dried up. Paul was still patting her shoulder with an arthritic old hand as she wiped away the last of her tears. "I know my Michael was hard and cruel with us in the last few years," she said, blowing her nose on a silk handkerchief, "but he was still my boy, Paul. He was still my boy."

Was? Tilly decided not to ask, but went on sweeping the floors, staying close in case they needed something.

"I know, my love." Paul shakily kissed Aggie's forehead. "But pull yourself together now. We have to arrange all of the details." He looked up. "Tilly, my dear girl, please come and sit here. We have something we must discuss with you."

Tilly returned obediently to the table. "Yes, sir?"

Paul leaned forward, staring down at his hand. "Our son, Michael..." He paused, clearing his throat. "Michael died from cholera last week. That man was his solicitor... apparently Michael was not married and left no will. We are his closest living relatives... he had something of an estate, it seems."

"I'm so sorry to hear he's gone," said Tilly.

"He was a bad boy," said Aggie faintly. "He didn't care for anyone other than himself, and it was that school that did it. He was such a caring little boy before he went there." She wiped at fresh tears, gazing out of the kitchen window at the laughing children in the field. "Used to be so much like your dear little Robby."

"Now, now, Aggie," said Paul softly. He turned back to Tilly. "The solicitor wants us to go into London for the day tomorrow, to attend to some urgent matters with regards to his estate. I know it's very near to Christmas, but we shall have no choice but to drive into the city tomorrow morning, attend to the estate, spend the night, and then drive back the next day."

Tilly nodded. "Don't worry," she said. "I'll make sure everything is well here on the farm."

The couple exchanged a glance. "Actually, Tilly," said Paul gently, "we're going to ask Ian from next door to watch over the farm. We need someone to come with us... someone who knows the city well and will be able to help us."

"Oh, dearest Tilly, please do come with us," said Aggie. "I hate the city. It's so big and frightening... but I know we would be all right with you there."

Tilly stared at them for a second, utterly aghast. Go back to London? The city that had taken everything she loved? She knew that Bert would never hurt anyone again, but what if there were other men in London like him? London was cursed for her; Tilly was sure of it.

But looking into Paul and Aggie's kind eyes, Tilly couldn't say no to them. They had given her so much – every shred of happiness she had now was as a result of their kindness. How could she ignore that?

"All right, of course," she said. "I'll go with you. If Ian keeps an eye on everything, Janie will take care of her younger siblings, and they'll be all right."

"Oh, Tilly, you angel." Aggie leaned over, clasping Tilly's hands in both of hers. "You sweet, sweet thing. Thank you."

Tilly forced a smile, a pit of dread opening in her stomach. She couldn't get this London trip over with quickly enough.

CHAPTER 19

TILLY HAD NEVER SEEN SUCH a picture-perfect winter's day. She couldn't admit to herself that some part of her had missed the abundance of decorations on the streets of London at this time of year, but she had: nowhere in the country would the streets be so thickly draped with bunting and evergreens, the windows glow with quite so many candles, the doors and walls be so covered in wreaths. There were Christmas trees outside on the streets too, and as the hired carriage rumbled through a still and empty market square, Tilly saw yet another group of carollers. They had passed three since leaving the inn on their way out of London. These were mostly children, all dressed in long white and gold robes and carrying tall candles. The air was so still that the flames didn't move at all; snow was tumbling down in a soft, white curtain, and the children's voices carried far, pure and piping as the familiar carol filled the air.

Silent night. Mystical night.

Purple dome, starry light.

Pouring splendour of centuries down,

gold and purple, a glorious crown,

where the manger so rude and wild

cradles a sleeping child.

Their music was beautiful, and despite the worry that had been building in Tilly's chest ever since she'd first laid eyes on the city yesterday, she could relax and enjoy it a little now that they were safely on their way. Soon, London would lie far behind her, where it belonged, and she would be back in that cosy cottage on the farm with her children, her comfort, and her growing loneliness.

Part of her didn't want to leave the city. She tried to ignore it, but it wouldn't let her stop scanning through the faces of every happy band of revellers they passed.

"Tilly, my dear, won't you close the window?" Aggie asked.

Tilly didn't want to. She wanted to keep on searching, keep on staring into the crowds, but how could she explain her forlorn hope to Aggie? She smiled, swinging the window shut and sitting down again opposite Aggie and Paul in the back of the carriage.

"Are you enjoying the sight of London again, Tilly?" asked Paul.

Tilly forced a smile. "I'll be glad to get back to the country."

"It seems as though you're looking for something," said Aggie.

Tilly looked away. The couple had experienced a hard day yesterday. Aggie was mourning Michael even though he had been so cruel to her, and they had spent hours at the solicitor's office, trying to sort out Michael's estate. She didn't want to burden them with the strange ache in her chest.

But she'd underestimated Aggie's shrewdness. The old woman was looking at her with a beady eye. "You *are* looking for something, aren't you?" she said. "Or someone, perhaps."

Tilly looked at her, surprised.

"I know you're a widow," said Aggie, "but I also know you left someone behind here in this city. The children tell me about him sometimes. Micah, I think?"

"Yes, ma'am," Tilly admitted. Her cheeks warmed. "After my husband was presumed dead, there was a young man who helped me very much. We were going to be married, and then Ray came home after two years lost on an island."

"What happened to this Micah?" Aggie asked.

"I don't know." Tilly gazed out of the window again. "I saw him just before Ray died. He seemed... happy, I suppose. I... I didn't ask very much. That was the last time I ever saw him."

"He sounds like a good man," said Aggie. "The children loved him."

Tilly couldn't stop the truth from escaping her. "*I* loved him."

The carriage rattled on. They were out of earshot of the carollers now, and Tilly felt a sharp desperation to get out of London and back to the farm. It was time she forgot about Micah, yet every time she tried, he seemed to have an unbreakable grip on her heart.

"What work did this Micah do?" asked Paul, in a deep grunt.

Tilly looked at him, surprised, but his expression was unreadable.

"He was an ironsmith, sir. He worked out of his flat on Shetland Street," she said. "But that was many years ago."

Paul grunted, losing interest in the conversation. He rapped on the side of the carriage. "Stop, please," he called, got out, and conferred with the driver for a few moments. Aggie opened the book she'd brought with her to keep herself occupied on the journey, and Tilly went on staring out of the window as Paul returned and the carriage rumbled on.

She wondered what would have happened if Ray had never come back. Would she and Micah be married? Or would Bert have killed Micah instead? London was bogging her down in all of its many sorrows again. Tilly closed her eyes, hoping to fall asleep for a little while. She just wanted to go home now.

But when they bumped to a halt, it was much too soon; Tilly hadn't slept at all, and they couldn't possibly have left London yet. She sat up, blinking at Aggie and Paul. "Are you two all right, sir, ma'am?" she asked.

"Quite all right," said Paul. "Tell me, Tilly, is this the right Shetland Street?"

Tilly couldn't believe her ears. Much less could she believe her eyes when she looked out of the window and was struck by an unbelievably familiar sight. A row of small brick bungalows, no gardens, a narrow street; and halfway down, a house that she found breathtakingly familiar. A house she had once hoped to live in.

The house in which Micah had proposed to her.

Her heart was thundering in her mouth. She looked at Paul with wide eyes.

"Go on, then," said Paul. "Knock on the door. See if he's here."

"I – " Tilly could hardly breathe. "I can't."

"You must, my darling, you must." Aggie was pushing the door open, practically shoving Tilly out of it. "You will always regret it if you don't."

Tilly knew it was true, but she was still shaking all over as she walked up to that door, her heart racing, her breath catching. What if he'd moved? What if his pretty new wife opened the door? What if he didn't remember her? What...

She looked back. Aggie grinned at her. Almost for their sake instead of her own, Tilly knocked.

The door opened, and there he was. Perfect as the day she'd first met him selling pots on a street corner in her most desperate hour. Only she wasn't desperate now, and he was still the most wonderful thing she'd ever laid eyes on, from his corkscrew curls to his big, warm smile. It faltered when he looked down at her, his eyes widening, his big hands falling limply to his sides. He was wearing nice clothes; pressed black trousers, a sturdy white shirt with a little bowtie and suspenders. He looked too wonderful to express.

"Hello, Micah," Tilly managed huskily.

The surprise melted from his features, turning into joy. "Tilly," he said. "Oh – I'm so glad to see you. I've been wondering about you ever since I read about Ray in the papers."

That had been three years ago. And he had read about the tragedy. He remembered her. Of course, he remembered her.

"You look so well," Micah said. He stepped toward her, reached for her as if to touch her, then dropped his hands to his sides again. He wore no wedding ring. "How are the children?"

"Better. Much better." Tilly swallowed, hating the stilted feel of their conversation. "We live in the country now. My employers had to come to London, and... and they stopped by for me... to see you."

They stared at one another for a long, long moment. But Tilly could hold back no more. She took a small step closer, just enough that she could smell him, his uniqueness, the cinnamon sort of edge to his scent, and it gave her courage.

"Micah, I've missed you so much," she said, holding out her hands to him.

A slow grin spread over his features, strong and perfect. He took her hands in his own, folding his strong fingers over hers, and it was as though he had never let go. She knew every cranny and crevice of his grip. It was home to her.

"And I've missed you, Tilly," he said. A happy tear escaped, running down his cheek. "Oh, how I've missed you. I couldn't dare hope... I couldn't, well..."

He began to laugh, and then she was laughing too, smiling up into his eyes, allowing herself at last to lower the floodgates that had been holding back her feelings and allow an overflow of emotions to rush through her. She knew then her love had not been dormant but had been growing quietly under the surface ever since she first laid eyes on Micah.

He was telling her now about how his business had grown, and how he was about to buy a shop of his own, and how he'd gone to her cottage over and over again after Ray had died, hoping to see her, to help her somehow, but that she had never been home. She told him how she had moved to the country, and that Lissa was playing piano, and Janie was reading whole novels now.

"Novels?" Micah laughed with joy. "Oh, Tilly, that is wonderful – that is so, so wonderful." He squeezed her hands, his eyes sparkling. "I... I would love to see them, sometime."

Tilly glanced over her shoulder at Aggie, who was watching eagerly from the carriage and nodded violently.

"Well, Micah, I..." She looked up at him, realizing that she had never been more sure of anything in her life. "I wonder if you would like to come on Christmas Day? It's not far from here; I'll write down some directions for you. You could come out for lunch, stay the night, and get home on Boxing Day."

Micah's grin split his face, made all of Christmas itself seem brighter.

"Yes, I would like that," he said. "I would like that very much."

"You'll come?" said Tilly, half afraid to believe it.

He looked as though he might kiss her then, and Tilly wanted him to, with everything in her. But with Aggie and Paul right there, he didn't.

"I'll be there," he said. "I promise."

THE LAST PROMISE that had been made to Tilly had been gruesomely broken. She tried not to think of that as she tucked the roast goose back into the oven, hoping to keep it warm. The kitchen was all ready for Christmas lunch; there were crackers on the table, paper chains hanging from every surface, thick bouquets of holly and mistletoe in the centre, a set of Advent candles burning brightly on one end. Everything was ready. Aggie and Paul had been wonderfully generous for the past few years in inviting Tilly and the children to join them for Christmas lunch, let alone Micah. All week, they'd been talking about seeing him at Christmas.

But no one was as excited to see him as the children. Lissa was squirming in place where she sat on her stool in front of the hearth, wide-eyed at the gigantic plum pudding on the kitchen table. "When is he coming, Mama?" she asked plaintively. "It's past one o' clock already."

"I don't know," said Tilly, her heart wrenching. Had he meant anything he'd said?

"He'll come," said Janie. She put a hand on Tilly's shoulder. "Don't worry, Mama. He'll come."

"I hope he brings a donkey," said Robby vaguely. "I like donkeys."

Tilly looked into Janie's eyes and was surprised at what she saw there. Janie was always the skeptic, always the cautious one, but her eyes right now were filled with utter faith.

"You think so?" she whispered.

"I know it. He'll be here," said Janie.

Her words were scarcely cold when the old dog barked in the farmyard, and the children flooded to the window with cries of joy. When Tilly threw the door open, Micah was just stepping down from his cart, with a strong young donkey in the harness. Micah's shoulders were dusted with snow, and his arms were full of brown parcels as he walked up to the front door, smiling from ear to ear.

"Merry Christmas, everyone," he boomed.

The children surged out of the door and threw their arms around him, chattering and clamouring, the parcels crashing accidentally to the ground, laughter filling the air as Micah and Tilly scrambled to retrieve them. And suddenly, just like that, all was well with the world.

***

It was late by the time Aggie and Paul finally went to bed, bringing an end to a glorious evening full of games and chatter. The children had eaten candy canes until they were nearly sick; Tilly herself was pleasantly full of fruitcake and gingerbread, and almost nauseous from endless laughter. They had played cards and charades and blind man's bluff, and with every moment, it had felt as though Micah belonged among them. As though he were already part of their family.

Now, Tilly was leading him across the farmyard to the loft where she had made up a bed for him. The children had already been put to bed in their cottage across the yard, and there were no lights on in the farmhouse, save the flicker of the Advent candles in the kitchen. The faint candlelight lit up the Christmas tree in the window, with its bright angel at the very top; the wreaths and bunting and holly shone in every window, and the sky was absolutely still and clear, with every star brilliant against the backdrop of deepest black. Tilly wondered if the first Christmas had been something like this. The sky could hardly have been any brighter, and her heart scarcely any happier, than if the whole host of angels had appeared singing about peace and goodwill.

They had been laughing and talking all night, but a peaceful silence settled around them now, like a warm blanket drawn close and bringing them together. Their steps matched perfectly, crunching on the powdery white snow that coated the cobbled yard. Tilly gazed up at Micah, at the way the silvery starlight kissed his high cheekbones, at the profusion of his black curls.

"I've been thinking," Micah said softly.

Tilly smiled. "About what?"

"Miracles," said Micah.

A cold wind found a way through Tilly's coat, making her shiver. Naturally, easily, Micah reached out and put an arm around her shoulders.

"Miracles?" said Tilly.

"Yes," said Micah. "People talk about them as though they always happen quickly, with fire and lightning, in a single, dazzling moment. But I don't think all miracles are like that. I don't even think all Christmas miracles are like that."

Tilly leaned against him, content to be so close to him. "Christmas doesn't last that long," she said softly.

"No, but its miracles do."

They had reached the barn door. Micah turned to face her, a smile dancing in his eyes, bright as Advent candles.

"What do you mean?" Tilly whispered, but she knew what he meant, for she saw it in his smile.

"I mean that some miracles grow slowly, quietly, like seeds beneath the ground," said Micah. "Some of them take root like trees, and wax and wane with the seasons, but they always live on. They're always there, ready to burst into fruit and ripen on a Christmas Day like this one."

Tilly knew he was right. She knew seasons changed, and hardship came and went. But some things lasted. And what she felt hanging in the air between them tonight was one of those things.

"Tilly, I've waited a long time to ask you this." Micah reached into his pocket, and he drew out the little cardboard box. "I know it's only been a few days since we found each other again, but I don't want to wait a moment longer. I think our Christmas miracle has come at last." He slipped down to one knee, holding out the little iron ring with its heart-shaped engraving. "You are my joy, my carol, my hope. Will you marry me?"

Tilly's heart was thundering wildly, beating almost out of her chest with happiness. She didn't know what the future held; she was sure that hard times lay ahead, just as they lay behind her. As beautiful as this Christmas was, it wouldn't bring about an end to all suffering.

But that was not the point of Christmas. The point of Christmas was not fulfilled joy, but hope: hope for family, for a brighter day coming, for the breaking of the dawn, for the coming of the summer, for a life coloured by both hardship and overwhelming love.

"Yes," she whispered. This time, nothing was holding her back. "Yes, yes, I will, I will."

He slipped the ring onto her finger, then rose to his feet, threw his arms around her waist and twirled her through the freezing air. Tilly's laugh echoed across the farmyard.

It was a truly merry Christmas at last.

The End

CONTINUE READING...

THANK you for reading ***The Forgotten Widow's Christmas!*** Why not read ***The Eight-Shilling Girl*** next? **Here's a sneak peek for you:**

Flora Clark's day began the same way every other day had begun for the past two years: with a burst of light filling the tiny room she shared with three other little girls.

"Time to get up," snapped a cold, shaky voice. "Come on, you lazy little wenches. Get up."

Flora opened her eyes. The brilliance of the naked gas lamp that illuminated the room seared across her exhausted eyes. In reality, she knew she must have had four or five hours of sleep, but it felt as though she'd barely had time to lie down on her lumpy straw mattress before the brutal wake-up call jerked her from her desperate slumber.

"Get up, I say," croaked Mrs. Haggis, the angry old cook who served as the taskmaster for the three little girls in the room – and the three bigger girls in the next one. "There's no time for this, you lay-abouts."

Flora was already stumbling across the room toward the rail on the far side where their black-and-white uniforms hung neatly in a row. The rail was the only tidy thing in the room; the rest of it was a chaos of mattresses and blankets, a place where there was no time for tidying up, or for anything else except sleeping. The other girls were rolling to their feet, yawning and blinking as Mrs. Haggis continued to shout at them all. Flora tried not to think about how her limbs ached as she reached up to take her uniform carefully off the wall. Soiling it, and thus causing extra work to be done, would be punishable by a slap from Mrs. Haggis.

When Flora pulled off her nightie over her head, Mrs. Haggis took this as her cue to leave and slammed the door behind her, sending dust pluming out of the bare wood. Flora's flesh was instantly goose-pimpled in the cold air. The girls' room was down in the basement of the Great Hotel, right in the icy bowels of the earth, and even though winter had recently faded from the city, it seemed as though its ghost still lingered in the air down here.

It was a relief to pull her crisp uniform over her head and tie the apron snugly around her thin waist. Stifling a yawn, she flattened down her hair, squashing a white bonnet over her ears.

"Come on, Liza," said one of the other girls. "We'll all be beaten if you're late."

"But I'm so tired," Liza complained. She was a couple of years older than Flora; perhaps thirteen or fourteen. "My feet hurt."

"All of our feet hurt," said the other girl, Olive. "It doesn't matter to nobody. More of us will hurt if we don't get going."

Flora knew that Olive was right; if one of the girls was late, Mrs. Haggis would be angry all day.

Click Here to Continue Reading!

https://www.ticahousepublishing.com/victorian-romance.html

THANKS FOR READING

IF YOU **LOVE** VICTORIAN ROMANCE, **Click Here**

https://victorian.subscribemenow.com/

to hear about all **New Faye Godwin Romance Releases! I will let you know as soon as they become available!**

Thank you, Friends! If you enjoyed ***The Forgotten Widow's Christmas,*** would you kindly take a couple minutes to leave a positive review on Amazon? It only takes a moment, and positive reviews truly make a difference. Thank you so much! I appreciate it!

Much love,

Faye Godwin

MORE FAYE GODWIN VICTORIAN ROMANCES!

We love rich, dramatic Victorian Romances and have a library of Faye Godwin titles just for you! (Remember that ALL of Faye's Victorian titles can be downloaded FREE with Kindle Unlimited!)

CLICK HERE to discover Faye's Complete Collection of Victorian Romance!

https://ticahousepublishing.com/victorian-romance.html

ABOUT THE AUTHOR

Faye Godwin has been fascinated with Victorian Romance since she was a teen. After reading every Victorian Romance in her public library, she decided to start writing them herself —which she's been doing ever since. Faye lives with her husband and young son in England. She loves to travel throughout her country, dreaming up new plots for her romances. She's delighted to join the Tica House Publishing family and looks forward to getting to know her readers.

contact@ticahousepublishing.com

Printed in Great Britain
by Amazon

57612414R00126